STORIES IN TIME

STATES
AND
REGIONS

ACTIVITY BOOK

HARCOURT BRACE & COMPANY

Orlando Atlanta Austin Boston San Francisco Chicago Dallas

New York Toronto London

Requests for permission to make copies of any part of the work or for information on licenses to duplicate this work should be mailed to: School Permissions Department, Harcourt Brace & Company, 6277 Sea Harbor Drive, Orlando, Florida 32887–6777.

HARCOURT BRACE and Quill Design is a registered trademark of Harcourt Brace & Company.

For permission to reprint copyrighted material, grateful acknowledgment is made to the following sources:

Columbia University Press: From "Spring River" (Retitled: "The Chang Jiang") by Po Chü-i in *The Columbia Book of Chinese Poetry,* translated and edited by Burton Watson. Text copyright © 1984 by Columbia University Press.

HarperCollins Publishers: From "The Nile" in *Atlas and Beyond* by Elizabeth J. Coatsworth. Text copyright © 1924 by Harper & Brothers; text copyright © renewed 1952 by Elizabeth Coatsworth.

Alfred A. Knopf, Inc.: From *They Live by the Wind* by Wendell P. Bradley. Text copyright © 1966, 1969 by Helen B. Henry, Edward Bradley, and John P. Bradley.

William L. Terry: From "Down the Mississippi" in *Selected Poems* by John Gould Fletcher. Text copyright 1938 by John Gould Fletcher; text copyright © 1966 by Charlie May Fletcher.

Printed in the United States of America

ISBN 0-15-303572-2

1 2 3 4 5 6 7 8 9 10 085 99 98 97 96

The activities in this book reinforce or extend social studies concepts and skills in **STATES AND REGIONS.** There is one activity for each lesson and skill. Reproductions of the activity pages appear with answers in the Teacher's Edition.

CONTENTS

POSTCARDS
to Fanny

Imagine that Robert Louis Stevenson sent postcards to his sweetheart, Fanny, during his trip across America.

Identify Landforms

DIRECTIONS: Use what you know about landforms in the United States to complete the messages on these two postcards.

Dear Fanny,

As this card shows, my train is passing through the

_____ .

I wish you could see this part of the country. I'll try to describe it for you.

The land is _____

_____ .

Get well soon.
Robert

Dear Fanny,
After passing through the Rocky Mountains, we're here in the

_____ .

I have never seen land like this. It is

_____

_____

Besides the desert, there are mountains, valleys,

_____ ,

and _____ .

I will see you soon.
Robert

NAME _____ DATE _____

THE COLUMBIA RIVER SYSTEM

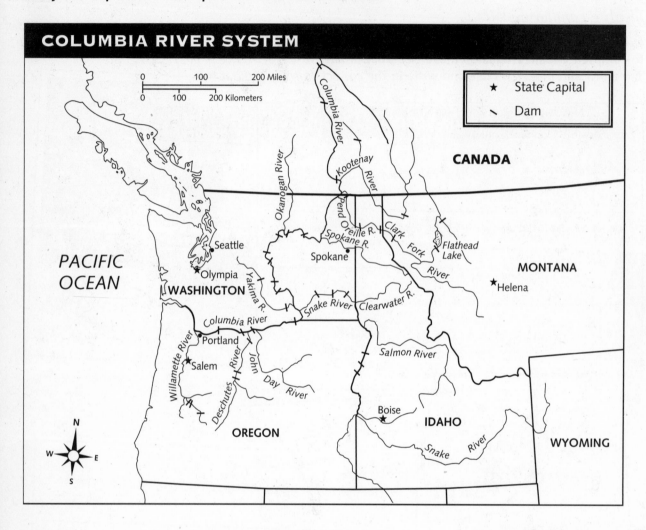 *Map Skill* *Locate Features on a Map*

DIRECTIONS: The map below shows the Columbia River system.
Study the map and then complete the activities that follow.

1. Trace the path of the Columbia River in blue.

2. Put an **X** at the source of the Columbia River.

3. Put a **Y** at the mouth of the Columbia River.

4. Use another color to trace the path of the Snake River, a major tributary of the Columbia River.

5. Underline the names of the other rivers in Oregon that are part of the Columbia River system.

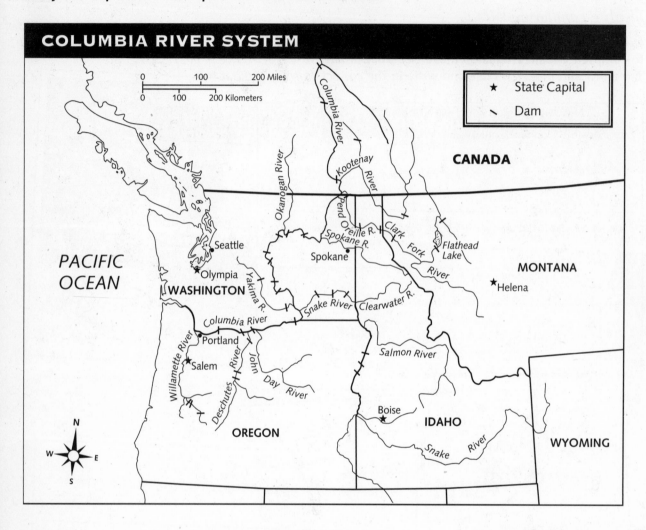

Use after reading Chapter 1, Lesson 2, pages 44–49.

HOW TO USE AN Elevation Map

Apply Map Skills

DIRECTIONS: Study this elevation map, and read each sentences below. Circle T if the sentence is true and F if the sentence is false. If the sentence is false, cross out the word that makes it false and write in the correct word to make it true.

1. Lubbock is higher than Corpus Christi.   T   F

2. The highest parts of Texas are located in the south.   T   F

3. Most of Texas lies below sea level.   T   F

4. Brownsville is lower than Austin.   T   F

5. The Brazos River flows in a southeast direction.   T   F

6. Austin and San Antonio are found in the same   T   F
   range of elevations.

Use after reading Chapter 1, Skill Lesson, pages 50–51.

Climate Check

Analyze Data from Tables

DIRECTIONS: The tables below show average monthly temperatures (in degrees Fahrenheit) and precipitation (in inches) for three cities. Use this information to answer the questions below.

ANCHORAGE, ALASKA

	JAN	FEB	MAR	APRIL	MAY	JUNE	JULY	AUG	SEPT	OCT	NOV	DEC
Temperature	12	18	23	35	46	54	58	56	48	35	21	14
Precipitation	0.8	0.8	0.6	0.6	0.6	1.0	1.9	2.2	2.5	1.5	1.0	1.0

DUBUQUE, IOWA

	JAN	FEB	MAR	APRIL	MAY	JUNE	JULY	AUG	SEPT	OCT	NOV	DEC
Temperature	19	23	34	48	60	69	74	72	63	52	37	25
Precipitation	1.4	1.3	2.4	3.2	4.1	4.5	3.9	3.6	4.0	2.6	2.0	1.6

PHOENIX, ARIZONA

	JAN	FEB	MAR	APRIL	MAY	JUNE	JULY	AUG	SEPT	OCT	NOV	DEC
Temperature	52	56	61	68	76	85	91	89	84	72	60	53
Precipitation	0.7	0.7	0.7	0.3	0.1	0.1	0.9	0.1	0.8	0.5	0.6	0.9

1. Which city is warmest in December? _____

2. Which city is coolest in July? _____

3. Describe the climate in Dubuque during March and April.

_____

4. Which city has the driest climate? _____

5. Which city has the wettest climate? _____

6. Based on climate, which city would you like to live in? Explain your answer on a separate sheet of paper.

HELP WANTED

People often do work based on the kind of resources available in their region. The table on the right lists some of the resources, products, or industries of several states. The "jobs offered" chart on the left lists different jobs.

Make Connections

DIRECTIONS: Match each job with the state where it is likely to be commonly offered. Write the letter of the correct state in the box to the left of each job.

JOBS OFFERED

1. Fish canner

2. Miner

3. Subway car designer

4. Paper mill worker

5. Cheese maker

6. Cloth maker

7. Computer programmer

8. Fruit juice packager

9. Oil-pipeline builder

STATE INFORMATION

STATE	SOME RESOURCES, PRODUCTS, OR INDUSTRIES
a. Texas	Service industries, electronic equipment
b. Alaska	Oil, natural gas
c. Maine	Timber, forestry, paper pulp
d. West Virginia	Coal, gravel, crushed stone
e. Wisconsin	Dairy farming
f. Washington	Rivers, ocean ports, fishing
g. Florida	Oranges, grapefruit
h. Ohio	Transportation equipment, machinery
i. South Carolina	Cotton

Harcourt Brace School Publishers

HOW TO USE a Land Use and Resource Map

Here is a map of the imaginary state of East Albion. Instead of using different colors to show land use, this map uses other kinds of symbols, including picture symbols. This map also uses picture symbols to show the state's leading resources as well as some of its major crops.

Apply Map Skills

DIRECTIONS: Use what you know about land use and resource maps and map symbols to fill in the missing information in the map key.

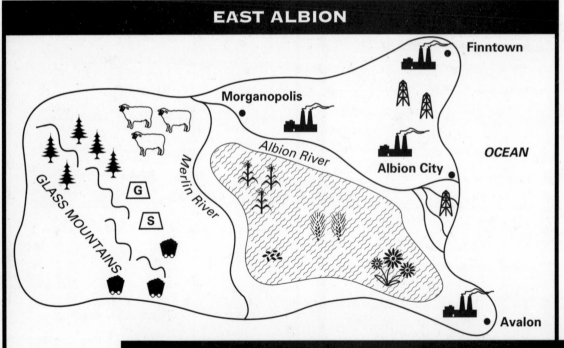

EAST ALBION

Finntown

Morganopolis

Albion River

OCEAN

Albion City

GLASS MOUNTAINS

Merlin River

G

S

Avalon

MAP KEY

LAND USE	LEADING RESOURCES	MAJOR CROPS
🌲 _____	▲ Coal	🌽 _____
🐑 _____	G Gold	🌾 _____
▨ _____	S Silver	Soybeans
🏭 _____	⚒	Flowers

Harcourt Brace School Publishers

Use after reading Chapter 1, Skill Lesson, pages 62–63.

• THE DISAPPEARING LAND

The terrible dust storms of the 1930s made people throughout the United States more aware of their environment.

Analyze a Viewpoint

DIRECTIONS: Read this passage taken from Stuart Chase's 1936 book, Rich Land, Poor Land.

> A dust desert is forming east of the Rockies where firm grass once stood.
>
> One hundred million acres of formerly cultivated land has been essentially ruined by water erosion—an area equal to Illinois, Ohio, North Carolina, and Maryland combined. Erosion by wind and water is getting under way on another 100 million acres. More than 300 million acres—one-sixth of the country—is gone, going, or beginning to go.
>
> In times of low water, the pollution of streams becomes an ominous menace. In uncounted streams, fish lie killed by the wastes of cities and the black refuse of mine and factory. Pollution has destroyed more fish than all the fishermen.
>
> Besides the material and financial loss . . . , an environment lovely to the eye has been sacrificed.

DIRECTIONS: Using the passage you read and your own ideas, answer the following questions on a separate sheet of paper.

1. What message was Stuart Chase giving the people of the United States?

2. What is one example of natural damage to the environment that Chase uses to support his point of view?

3. What is one example of human damage to the environment that Chase uses to support his point of view?

4. If Stuart Chase were writing about the environment today, what signs of improvement would he see? In what ways would things be worse?

5. Do you think Stuart Chase believes the beauty of the environment is as important as its usefulness? Explain.

Use after reading Chapter 1, Lesson 5, pages 64–67.

ACTIVITY BOOK 7

Harcourt Brace School Publishers

The American Landscape

Connect Main Ideas

DIRECTIONS: Use this organizer to show that you understand how the chapter's main ideas are connected. Complete the organizer by writing three examples for each main idea.

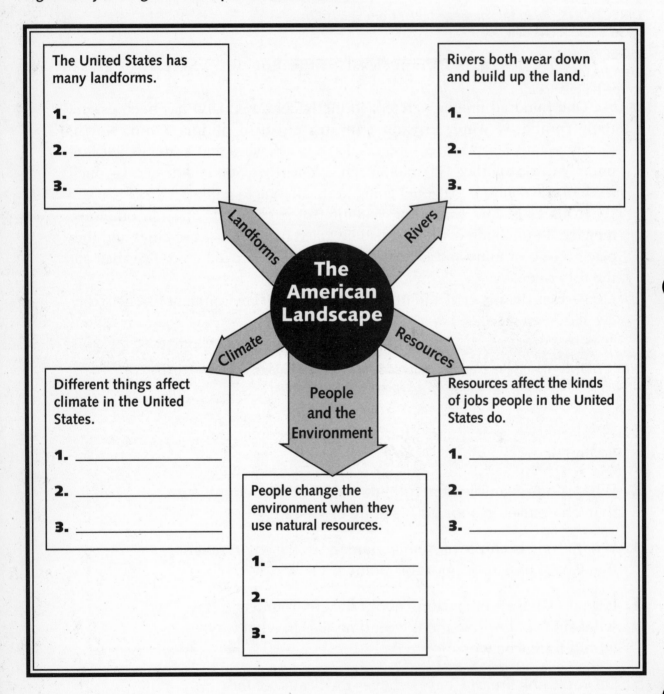

The United States has many landforms.

1. _____

2. _____

3. _____

Rivers both wear down and build up the land.

1. _____

2. _____

3. _____

Landforms

Rivers

The American Landscape

Climate

Resources

People and the Environment

Different things affect climate in the United States.

1. _____

2. _____

3. _____

People change the environment when they use natural resources.

1. _____

2. _____

3. _____

Resources affect the kinds of jobs people in the United States do.

1. _____

2. _____

3. _____

Use after reading Chapter 1, pages 38–69.

Welcome to America

This table shows the numbers of immigrants from each continent who came to the United States in a recent year.

Read and Create Bar Graphs

DIRECTIONS:
Use the information in the table to color the bars on the graph below.

IMMIGRANTS TO THE UNITED STATES

CONTINENT	NUMBER OF IMMIGRANTS
Africa	27,000
Asia	357,000
Australia	2,000
Europe	145,000
North America	384,000
South America	55,000
Total 1992 Immigration	**970,000**

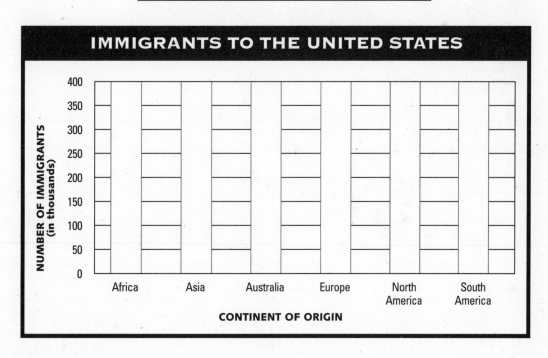

IMMIGRANTS TO THE UNITED STATES

Harcourt Brace School Publishers

(Continued)

This bar graph shows where immigrants settled in the United States in 1992.

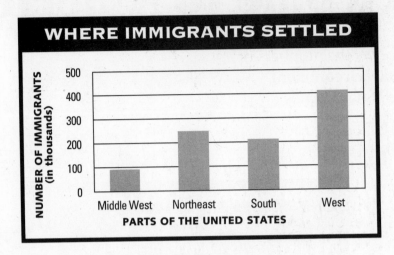

DIRECTIONS: *Use the information on this activity's table and bar graphs to answer the following questions.*

1. Which continent did the most immigrants come from?

_____

2. Which continent did the least number of immigrants come from, Africa or South America?

_____

3. How many immigrants came from Asia?

_____

4. Which part of the United States became home to the most immigrants?

_____

5. Why do you think more immigrants settled in the Northeast and West than in the

Middle West and South? _____

_____

_____

_____

Use after reading Chapter 2, Lesson 1, pages 71–75.

HOW TO MAKE a Thoughtful Decision

Learning to make choices is like choosing which direction to go at a crossroads.

Apply Thinking Skills

DIRECTIONS: Read the situations below. For each situation, list two possible choices. For each choice, list two possible consequences.

- You are saving money for summer camp. A friend asks you to go to a new amusement park. This will cost all the money you have saved.

  Choice 1 _____

  Consequence _____

  Consequence _____

  Choice 2 _____

  Consequence _____

  Consequence _____

- You have a chance to take music lessons on Saturdays. A computer class is being offered at the same time. You really like music, but all your friends are signing up for the computer class.

  Choice 1 _____

  Consequence _____

  Consequence _____

  Choice 2 _____

  Consequence _____

  Consequence _____

DIRECTIONS: Now look over the consequences for each choice. For each situation, circle what you think is the better choice.

Harcourt Brace School Publishers

New Land, New Choices ●

Complete a Table

DIRECTIONS: Nary's life changed when he came to the United States. In the table below, use words or drawings to describe your favorite foods and favorite holiday. Then answer the question that follows.

	NARY IN CAMBODIA	NARY IN THE UNITED STATES	YOUR FAVORITE
Foods	Many Cambodian people eat rice with fish and vegetables.	Nary enjoys pizza and ice cream.	
Holidays	Cambodians celebrate the Water Festival in October or November, with boat races on the Tonle Sap.	Nary celebrates the birthday of the United States on the Fourth of July.	

Which of your favorite things would be most difficult to leave behind if you

had to move to a new country? Explain your answer. _____

_____

Use after reading Chapter 2, Lesson 2, pages 77–81.

"The Star-Spangled Banner"

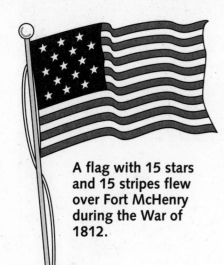

A flag with 15 stars and 15 stripes flew over Fort McHenry during the War of 1812.

During the War of 1812, Francis Scott Key stood on the deck of a ship, watching the English fire rockets and bombs at Fort McHenry, near Baltimore, Maryland. At dawn the next day, the American flag still flew over the fort. Key wrote a poem describing the battle.

Key's poem was set to music and became very popular. In 1931 the United States officially declared Key's song the National Anthem.

Use a Primary Source

DIRECTIONS: Read the first verse of "The Star-Spangled Banner." Then follow the instructions below.

Oh, say can you see by the dawn's early light
What so proudly we hail'd at the twilight's last gleaming,
Whose broad stripes and bright stars through the perilous fight
O'er the ramparts we watch'd were so gallantly streaming?
And the rockets' red glare, the bombs bursting in air,
Gave proof through the night that our flag was still there.
Oh, say does that star-spangled banner yet wave
O'er the land of the free and the home of the brave?

1. Many countries' national anthems celebrate battles and struggles. Underline the words in the first verse of "The Star-Spangled Banner" that describe the Battle of Fort McHenry.

2. The "banner" in the song is the American flag. Circle all the words in the first verse that describe the American flag.

3. Two words in this verse describe the people of the United States. Find these two words and underline them twice.

4. On a separate sheet of paper, draw your idea of what Francis Scott Key saw on the night of the battle, or write a short poem or song about an experience that made you feel proud to be an American.

Harcourt Brace School Publishers

NAME _____ DATE _____

HOW TO UNDERSTAND National Symbols

Apply Thinking Skills

DIRECTIONS: Each of the symbols shown below stands for ideas or qualities that people in the United States admire. Write the correct letter for each symbol on the line next to its meaning.

A. Independence Hall

B. The United States Capitol

C. The Bald Eagle

D. The White House

E. Gateway Arch

F. The Washington Monument

Meanings

_____ **1.** Honors the leadership of the nation's first President

_____ **2.** Stands for freedom; leaders meeting there on July 4, 1776, declared our country's independence from English rule

_____ **3.** Represents democracy and the freedom to elect our leaders

_____ **4.** Symbolizes the Presidency

_____ **5.** Represents strength and freedom; chosen as the national bird in 1782

_____ **6.** Honors the bravery of the pioneers who settled the West

Use after reading Chapter 2, Skill Lesson, pages 86–87.

Harcourt Brace School Publishers

Branches of Government

Organize Information

DIRECTIONS: Fill in the blanks to complete this graphic outline of the United States government. If you need help, reread Chapter 2, Lesson 4, in your textbook.

LEGISLATIVE BRANCH

Known as _____

Made up of the _____

and the _____

Main Job:

_____

_____

EXECUTIVE BRANCH

Headed by _____

_____

Main job:

_____

_____

JUDICIAL BRANCH

Made up of the _____

The most important court in the country is the _____ ,

which has _____ judges,

called _____ .

Main Job:

_____

_____

Harcourt Brace School Publishers

WE, The Many People ●

Connect Main Ideas

DIRECTIONS: Use this organizer to show that you understand how the chapter's main ideas are connected. Complete the organizer by writing three examples for each main idea.

There are different ways of life in the United States.

1. _____

2. _____

3. _____

Different things help unite people living in the United States.

1. _____

_____

2. _____

_____

3. _____

_____

We, the Many People

The United States government unites the people in the 50 states.

1. _____

_____

_____

_____

2. _____

_____

3. _____

_____

WYOMING *Counties*

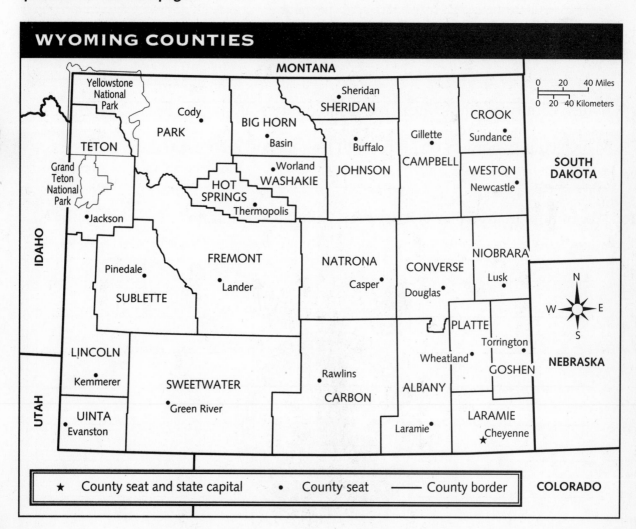

Identify Regions on a Map

DIRECTIONS: Most states are divided into smaller regions called counties. Each county has its own government. The city or town in which the county government is located is called the county seat. Use the information on the map to answer the questions on the next page.

WYOMING COUNTIES

MONTANA

Yellowstone National Park

Cody
PARK

Sheridan
SHERIDAN

CROOK
Sundance

0 20 40 Miles
0 20 40 Kilometers

TETON

BIG HORN
Basin

Gillette

CAMPBELL

Buffalo

WESTON
Newcastle

SOUTH DAKOTA

Grand Teton National Park

Worland
WASHAKIE

JOHNSON

Jackson

HOT SPRINGS
Thermopolis

IDAHO

FREMONT

Pinedale

Lander

SUBLETTE

NATRONA
Casper

CONVERSE
Douglas

NIOBRARA
Lusk

N
W   E
S

LINCOLN
Kemmerer

PLATTE
Torrington

Wheatland

GOSHEN

NEBRASKA

UTAH

SWEETWATER
Green River

Rawlins

CARBON

ALBANY

UINTA
Evanston

Laramie

LARAMIE
Cheyenne

★ County seat and state capital   • County seat   —— County border

COLORADO

(Continued)

1. What is the county seat of Goshen County? _____

2. What is the county seat of Hot Springs County? _____

3. Which county seat is also the state capital? _____

4. Which county is located in the northeast corner of the state?

   _____

5. Which county is located in the southwest corner of the state?

   _____

6. Which national park is located in the northwest corner of the state?

   _____

7. Which county is located in the southeast corner of the state?

   _____

8. Which county has the same name as its county seat? _____

9. Which county borders on both South Dakota and Nebraska?

   _____

10. About how many miles is it between Gillette and Buffalo?

   _____

Use after reading Chapter 3, Lesson 1, pages 97–101.

Harcourt Brace School Publishers

HOW TO USE LATITUDE and LONGITUDE

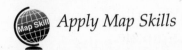 *Apply Map Skills*

DIRECTIONS: Below the map of Pennsylvania is a list of cities. Latitude and longitude coordinates are given for each city. If the coordinates show the latitude and longitude closest to the city, place a check mark in the space to the right. If the coordinates for the city are incorrect, write in the correct coordinates.

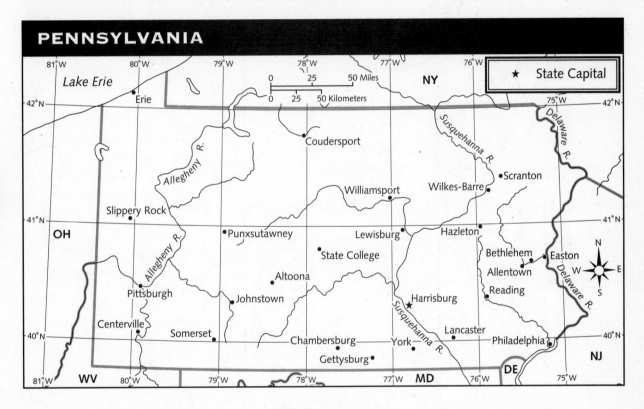

1. Erie (42°N/80°W) _____

2. Johnstown (42°N/78°W) _____

3. Philadelphia (42°N/77°W) _____

4. Pittsburgh (40°S/80°W) _____

5. State College (41°N/78°W) _____

6. Williamsport (40°N/78°W) _____

Harcourt Brace School Publishers

Use after reading Chapter 3, Lesson 1, pages 102–104.

Pieces of a Puzzle

Y̶ou have learned that regions of the United States can be described in many ways. All these ways of describing a region are like pieces of a puzzle.

Organize Information

DIRECTIONS: Describe the region where you live by filling in the information on each "puzzle piece." You may use words or drawings to describe your region. Exchange your finished work with a partner to see how someone else described the same region.

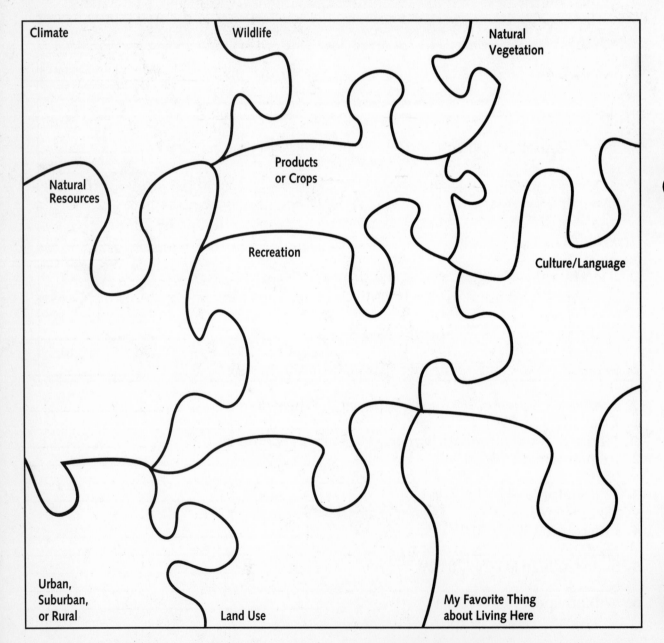

Climate

Wildlife

Natural Vegetation

Natural Resources

Products or Crops

Recreation

Culture/Language

Urban, Suburban, or Rural

Land Use

My Favorite Thing about Living Here

Are We There Yet?

Interstate highways link distant cities and regions of the United States. The map on the next page shows some of the major U.S. interstate highways. Highways that run east-west have even numbers. Highways that run north-south have odd numbers.

Map Skill *Read a Highway Map*

DIRECTIONS: Use the highway map on the next page to answer the questions below.

1. Which highway would take you from Los Angeles, California, to Portland,

   Oregon? _____

2. List two major cities along Interstate Highway 80. _____

   _____

3. Which highway connects Minnesota with Texas? _____

4. Tim's family lives in Maine. They want to tour the White House in Washington, D.C., visit relatives in Richmond, Virginia, and then vacation in Miami, Florida.

   Which highway should they take? _____

5. Which highway should you take if you want to start on the Pacific Coast, cross the Rocky Mountains, cross the Mississippi River, travel near three Great Lakes,

   and end up on the Atlantic Coast? _____

6. Which east-west interstate highway is the farthest south? _____

7. Interstate Highway 70 begins in Maryland. Where does it end? _____

8. Name the two interstate highways that cross Montana. _____

   _____

9. List three states through which Interstate Highway 40 passes.

   _____

   _____

(Continued)

INTERSTATE HIGHWAYS

ME

NH

VT

NY

MA

CT

RI

Boston

New York City

Philadelphia

Washington, D.C.

DE

MD

NJ

PA

Pittsburgh

Buffalo

90

80

90

70

95

WV

VA

Richmond

Charlotte

NC

SC

95

Jacksonville

Miami

FL

75

GA

Atlanta

70

TN

AL

Birmingham

MS

New Orleans

10

LA

AR

Little Rock

40

Memphis

KY

Cincinnati

75

OH

Cleveland

Detroit

Chicago

80

90

IN

70

IL

St. Louis

Mississippi

MO

Kansas City

Oklahoma City

40

Dallas

San Antonio

35

TX

10

MI

Milwaukee

75

WI

90

MN

Minneapolis

35

IA

Des Moines

Omaha

80

NE

90

KS

70

35

OK

40

ND

SD

ROCKY MOUNTAINS

MT

90

WY

80

25

Denver

CO

70

25

NM

Albuquerque

25

ID

15

Salt Lake City

15

UT

15

AZ

40

Phoenix

10

Seattle

90

WA

Portland

OR

5

NV

80

Sacramento

San Francisco

5

CA

15

Los Angeles

5

400 Miles

400 Kilometers

200

200

0

0

N E S W

Harcourt Brace School Publishers

Looking at Regions

Connect Main Ideas

DIRECTIONS: Use this organizer to show that you understand how the chapter's main ideas are connected. Complete the organizer by writing three examples for each main idea.

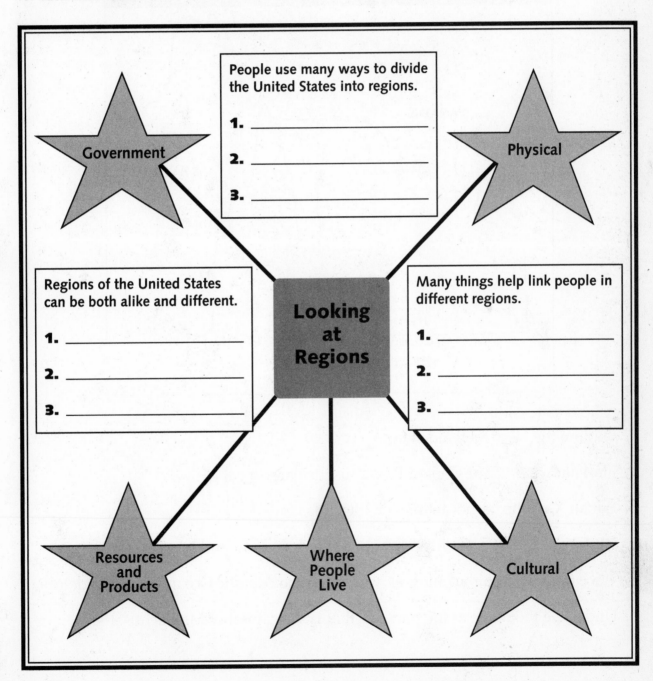

Government

People use many ways to divide the United States into regions.

1. _____

2. _____

3. _____

Physical

Regions of the United States can be both alike and different.

1. _____

2. _____

3. _____

Looking at Regions

Many things help link people in different regions.

1. _____

2. _____

3. _____

Resources and Products

Where People Live

Cultural

NAME _____ DATE _____

NORTHEAST Gateways

 Locate Features on a Map

DIRECTIONS: Use the map below. Then complete the activities that follow.

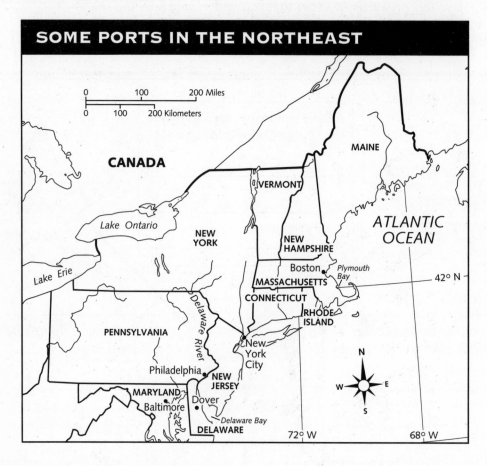

SOME PORTS IN THE NORTHEAST

1. Outline the New England states.

2. Find and circle Cape Cod—Massachusetts' largest cape.

3. Put an **X** on the harbor where the Pilgrims landed.

4. New York City is a port at the mouth of a river. Find and label that river.

5. Trace the path a ship would follow to reach the Atlantic Ocean from Philadelphia.

6. Underline the name of the port city that is the capital of Massachusetts.

Harcourt Brace School Publishers

Use after reading Chapter 4, Lesson 1, pages 131–135.

HOW TO READ a CUTAWAY Diagram

Apply Diagram Skills

DIRECTIONS: Look at the cutaway diagram of the Mayflower to tell which features are on the inside and which are on the outside. Fill in each blank below with an I if the feature is inside or an O if the feature is outside. Then answer the questions that follow.

_____ Water barrels   _____ Galley   _____ Upper deck

_____ Rudder   _____ Cargo hold   _____ Boat

_____ Pilgrims' quarters   _____ Forecastle   _____ Rigging

_____ Food hold   _____ Captain's cabin

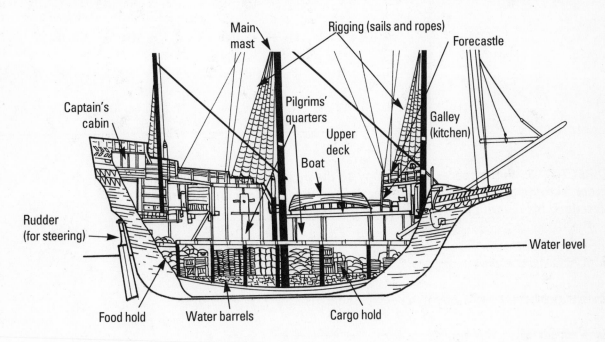

1. One feature labeled on the cutaway diagram is both outside and inside the ship. What is this feature? _____

2. The *Mayflower* voyage took more than two months. If you had to stay on this ship for more than two months, what would you find most difficult?

_____

Harcourt Brace School Publishers

A City Puzzle

Solve a Word Puzzle

DIRECTIONS: Find and circle terms from the Word Bank in the puzzle below. (Hint: All terms are printed across.)

WORD BANK

Ellis Island
Emma Lazarus
Lower East Side
Tri-State Region
tenements
Hartford
megalopolis

```
C I T T R I S T A T E R E G I O N Y
O E L L I S I S L A N D F S H I P S
O T H E B E A H A R T F O R D U T I
F U L O W E R E A S T S I D E L S H
M E G A L O P O L I S A R P B O W E
D S T E A M S H T E N E M E N T S I
P S A E M M A L A Z A R U S N D S A
I L S H I P S C I T Y O F T H E W O
R L D W A L T W H I T M A N P O E T
```

DIRECTIONS: In the spaces below, copy all the puzzle letters you did _not_ circle, in order, starting at the top left of the puzzle. You will see how one American described his favorite city, New York, in the 1860s.

— — — — — —   — —   — — — — — —!

— —   — — —   — — — — — — — — —

— — — — — —   -   — — — —   — — —

— — — — — — — — — —   — —

— — — —   — — — — — — — — — —!

— — — — —   — — — — — —!

—
— — — — —   — — — — — — —, — — — —

Use after reading Chapter 4, Lesson 2, pages 138–143.

Harcourt Brace School Publishers

HOW TO USE a Population Map

🌐 *Map Skill*

Apply Map Skills
   DIRECTIONS: The table
at the right gives recent population
densities for states in the Northeast.
Look at the map key on the next
page, and choose a different color
to fill each empty box in the key.
Then use the information in the
table to decide which color should
be used for each state. Color the
states to match the key. Then
answer the questions below.

STATE	POPULATION DENSITY (people per square mile)
Connecticut	957
Delaware	358
Maine	40
Maryland	508
Massachusetts	767
New Hampshire	126
New Jersey	1,062
New York	385
Pennsylvania	269
Rhode Island	676
Vermont	62

1. Which state in the Northeast has the lowest population density?

_____

2. Which state in the Northeast has the highest population density?

_____

3. New York is a large state, and it has the country's largest city. But New York's
population density is lower than that of several other states in the Northeast.

How is that possible? _____

_____

(Continued)

NORTHEAST POPULATION DENSITY

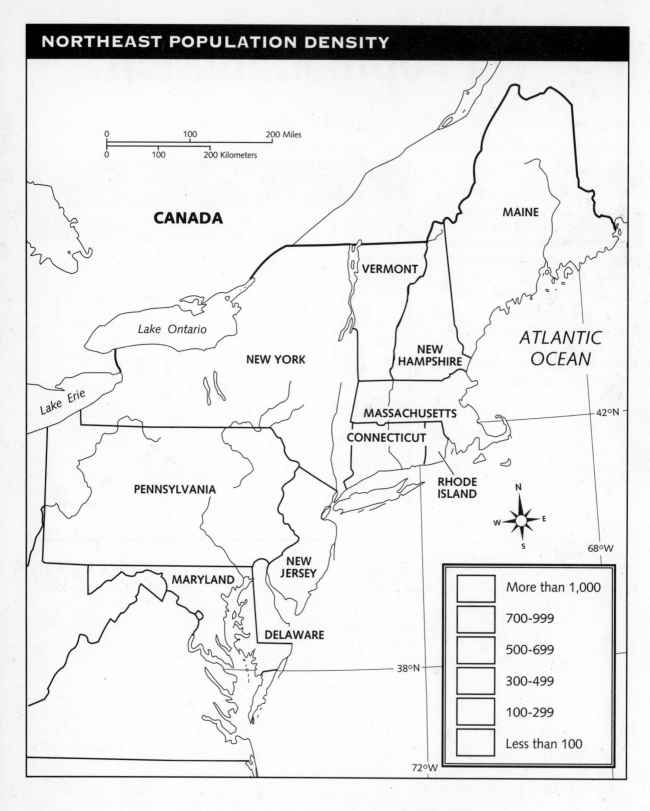

0   100   200 Miles

0   100   200 Kilometers

CANADA

MAINE

VERMONT

Lake Ontario

NEW YORK

NEW
HAMPSHIRE

ATLANTIC
OCEAN

Lake Erie

MASSACHUSETTS

CONNECTICUT

42°N

RHODE
ISLAND

N

W   E

S

68°W

PENNSYLVANIA

NEW
JERSEY

MARYLAND

DELAWARE

38°N

72°W

More than 1,000

700-999

500-699

300-499

100-299

Less than 100

Harcourt Brace School Publishers

DIRECTIONS: *Find New Jersey and Vermont on the map. On a separate sheet of paper, write a paragraph that describes how these two states might be different because of their different population densities.*

Use after reading Chapter 4, Skill Lesson, pages 146–147.

Your CITY of the FUTURE

Think Creatively

DIRECTIONS: *Imagine that you have been asked to design the ideal city of the future. On the "blueprints" below, draw or write one creative solution for each city problem.*

POLLUTION

TRAFFIC

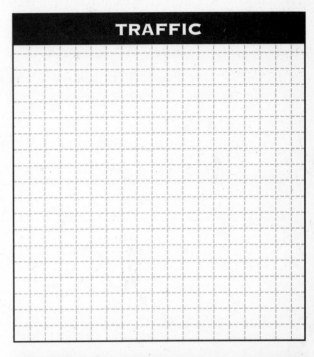

VIOLENCE

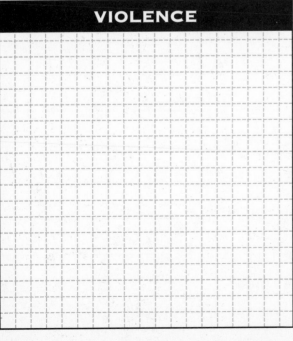

HIGH COST OF SERVICES

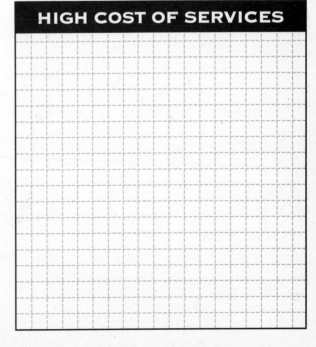

Use after reading Chapter 4, Lesson 3, pages 148–152.

HOW TO SOLVE a PROBLEM

Imagine that your class has a chance to go to a science fair in your state capital. The class will need five adult supervisors and will stay overnight. In order for the class to take part, it must raise enough money to pay for all the costs.

Apply Thinking Skills

DIRECTIONS: Use the questions below to think about and solve the problem, following the steps you learned in your textbook.

1. What is the biggest problem the class faces? _____

_____

_____

2. What is causing this problem? _____

_____

3. What seems to be the best way to solve this problem? _____

_____

4. How will you help? Who else can help? _____

_____

_____

5. How well do you think your solution will work? _____

_____

6. What other problems could make your solution fail? _____

_____

7. What can you try if your solution does not work? _____

_____

Use after reading Chapter 4, Skill Lesson, page 153.

Harcourt Brace School Publishers

NAME _____ DATE _____

Along the NORTHEAST coast

Connect Main Ideas

DIRECTIONS: Use this organizer to show that you understand how the chapter's main ideas are connected. Complete the organizer by writing three examples for each main idea.

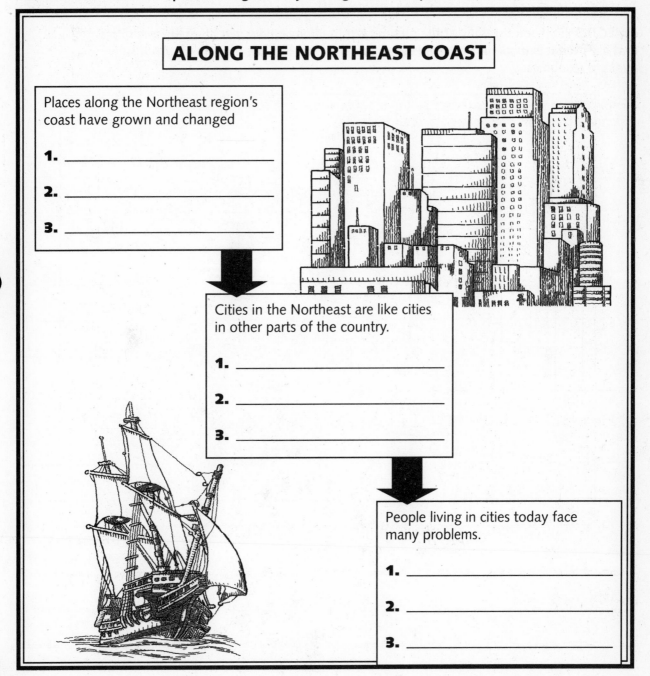

ALONG THE NORTHEAST COAST

Places along the Northeast region's coast have grown and changed

1. _____

2. _____

3. _____

Cities in the Northeast are like cities in other parts of the country.

1. _____

2. _____

3. _____

People living in cities today face many problems.

1. _____

2. _____

3. _____

A
NEW ENGLAND
PICNIC

Make Connections

DIRECTIONS: Look carefully at the picture. On the lines below, list all the picnic items that are products made in New England or are products that could be made from New England resources.

_____   _____

_____   _____

_____   _____

_____   _____

HOW **TO TELL** Fact from Opinion

Apply Thinking Skills

DIRECTIONS: Read the following passage, taken from a description of Vermont in the Time-Life book New England. Then follow the directions at the bottom of the page.

(1) Vermont has less level ground than almost any other state in the Union [United States]. Its people like to claim that (2) if Vermont were stamped flat, it would be bigger than Texas.

(3) Despite the terrain [the landforms] and generally poor soil, there was considerable farming at one time in Vermont, but the contour [hilliness] of the land was better suited to the scythe [a hand-held blade used for harvesting] than to mechanized equipment. (4) Late in the last century, long after such practices had been abandoned in the rest of New England, some Vermont farmers were still using oxen for work in the fields. The author Dorothy Canfield Fisher heard a Vermonter say of his native hills, (5) "What ought to be done with the old state is to turn it into a national park of a new kind—keep it just as it is, . . . so the rest of the country could come in to see how their grandparents lived."

DIRECTIONS: Decide whether each numbered statement gives a fact or an opinion. Write the numbers of the statements on the correct lines below. If you need help remembering how to tell the difference between a fact and an opinion, review page 161 of your textbook.

Fact _____

Opinion _____

Harcourt Brace School Publishers

Grand Banks Fishing

Read for Understanding

DIRECTIONS: The New England fishing industry has changed over the years. But the Grand Banks, which lie off the Atlantic coast of North America, remain one of the world's richest fishing areas. In They Live by the Wind, writer Wendell P. Bradley contrasts the old ways with the new ways. Read the passage below. Then, on a separate sheet of paper, answer the questions that follow.

In the late nineteenth century Gloucester [a city in Massachusetts] developed a fresh-fishing market, which centered around the old T warf in Boston. The fresh-fishing schooners had to race to market to beat rivals for the highest price and to keep their fish from spoiling.

The schooners were a delight and a source of pride to those who sailed them. Today that culture no longer exists. The . . . relationship to nature is changed. . . . Who can even catch a glimpse of its understanding of sea, weather, habits of different species of fish, techniques of catching fish, techniques of sailing? . . .

The mechanization [change to relying on mechanical instruments] of the fishing industry has wiped out the immense know-how of the fishermen of . . . New England. . . . Making a vessel go fast today is a matter of revving up the motor. Finding fish is done by turning on the fishscope, which enables the captain to see if fish are in the area. Finding your position is done with electronic equipment. . . . Storms are foretold not by the way clouds are making up to the northward, not by the wisdom inherited from generations of Grand Banks fishermen, but by Coast Guard weather reports.

1. Which way of fishing do you think the writer prefers?

2. Do you agree or disagree with him?

Harcourt Brace School Publishers

Use after reading Chapter 5, Lesson 2, pages 162–166.

CHANGING times

Organize Information

DIRECTIONS: Each of the statements below was true of one or more time periods in the Northeast's history. Read each statement. Then place the letter of the statement in the correct time-period box or boxes.

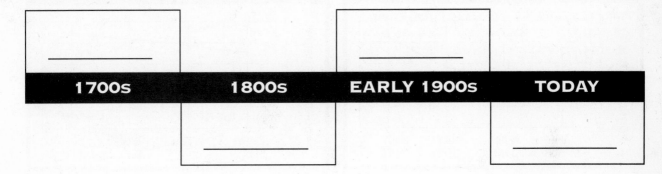

| 1700s | 1800s | EARLY 1900s | TODAY |

a. Railroads make it easier to move resources around the United States.

b. Most Americans till their own fields, build their own houses, and make what they need at home.

c. Amish people use horse-drawn plows and travel by horse and buggy.

d. The Northeast has a mostly agricultural economy.

e. The United States makes three-fifths of the world's steel.

f. Andrew Carnegie learns a better way to make steel.

g. Service industries are more important than manufacturing in the Middle Atlantic States.

h. Factory machines begin to run on steam and electricity.

i. The steel industry faces strong competition.

HOW TO USE a LINE Graph TO SEE CHANGE

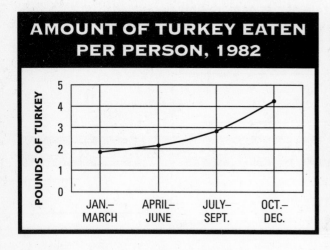

AMOUNT OF TURKEY EATEN PER PERSON, 1982

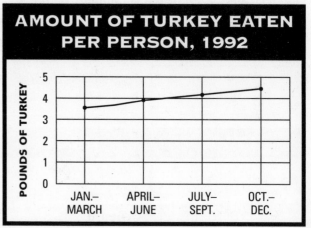

AMOUNT OF TURKEY EATEN PER PERSON, 1992

The Pilgrims, who settled in the Northeast, are associated in many peoples' minds with turkeys and Thanksgiving Day. Today, turkeys are raised in every Northeast state.

Apply Graph Skills

DIRECTIONS: Use the information in the line graphs above to answer these questions.

1. About how many pounds of turkey did each person eat between April and June

of 1982? _____

2. In one of the years shown, the amount of turkey eaten per person rose at a
fairly steady rate throughout the year. Which year was this?

_____

3. In which of the years shown did Americans eat less turkey?

_____

4. In which months of each year do Americans eat the most turkey?

_____ Why do you think this is?

_____

On the ERIE CANAL

People who piloted boats on the Erie Canal were called *canalers* (kuh•NAWL•uhrs). Mules walked on a towpath beside the canal and pulled the boats with ropes. Canalers had to stay awake all night to watch for locks. They made up songs about their work to pass the time. Here is one such song, called "Erie Canal."

I've got a mule, her name is Sal,
    Fifteen miles on the Erie Canal!
She's a good ol' worker and a good ol' pal
    Fifteen miles on the Erie Canal!
We've hauled some barges in our day,
    Filled with lumber and coal and hay,
And we know every inch of the way
    From Albany to Buffalo!

Chorus: Low bridge, everybody down!
          Low bridge, 'cause we're coming to a town,
          And you'll always know your neighbor,
          You'll always know your pal
          If you've ever navigated on the Erie Canal!

We'd better get along, old pal,
    Fifteen miles on the Erie Canal!
You can bet your life I'll never part from Sal,
    Fifteen miles on the Erie Canal!
Get up there, mule, here comes a lock!
    We'll make Rome by six o'clock;
One more trip, and back we'll go,
    Back we'll go to Buffalo.

Use a Source Document

DIRECTIONS: Use the information on this page, in the words of the song "Erie Canal," and in Lesson 4 of your textbook to answer the questions on the next page.

(Continued)

NAME _____ DATE _____

1. A repeated line in the song tells how many miles a canaler and his mule

   traveled on a typical journey. Write that line here. _____

   _____

2. Who is the singer's "pal" who helps him pull the barge?

   _____

3. What cargo does the singer haul on his barge? _____

   _____

4. What is a lock on a canal? _____

   _____

   _____

5. What New York town will the canaler reach by six o'clock?

   _____

6. What two cities did the Erie Canal connect? _____

   _____

7. What do you think the canaler means by the warning "Low bridge"?

   _____

   _____

   _____

8. Imagine that you are a canaler or a passenger on a canal boat. On the lines
   below, write a description of an interesting part of your journey.

   _____

   _____

   _____

   _____

   _____

Harcourt Brace School Publishers

• Using LAND and WATER

Connect Main Ideas

DIRECTIONS: Use this organizer to show that you understand how the chapter's main ideas are connected. Complete the organizer by writing three examples for each main idea.

USING LAND AND WATER

GEOGRAPHY	INTERACTION	CHANGE

Landforms and natural resources affect how people in New England live.	The Middle Atlantic states have changed because of the ways that people have used resources.	People have linked waterways in the Northeast to allow better transportation.
1. _____	1. _____	1. _____
_____	_____	_____
_____	_____	_____
2. _____	2. _____	2. _____
_____	_____	_____
_____	_____	_____
3. _____	3. _____	3. _____
_____	_____	_____
_____	_____	_____

COASTAL CROSSWORD

Solve a Word Puzzle

DIRECTIONS: Use the clues to complete the crossword. When you finish, read the letters inside the oval from top to bottom to see what the clues have in common.

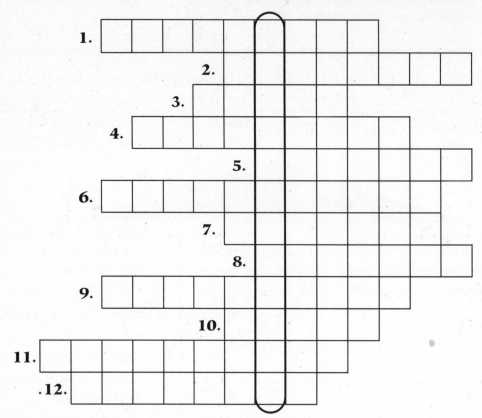

Clues

(1) A plant used to make sugar

(2) Indians who lived near the Atlantic Ocean in what is now Virginia

(3) A low, wet area where trees and bushes grow

(4) The first permanent English colony in North America

(5) Along with cotton, a crop grown to be sold for money

(6) Huge farms that were used for growing cotton, rice, or tobacco

(7) This state leads all others in growing citrus fruit.

(8) George Washington Carver found many uses for these.

(9) A large area of low, wet land in southern Florida.

(10) Low, wet land

(11) The average time between someone's birth and the birth of his or her children

(12) A farmer called this part of "America's greatest asset."

Use after reading Chapter 6, Lesson 1, pages 193–197.

From CROP to CLOSET

Follow a Sequence

DIRECTIONS: Read about how cloth is made from cotton. Then write the numbers from 1 to 8 in the blanks below to put the steps in the correct order.

When cotton is ready to pick, workers treat the plants with chemicals to remove the leaves. Then they use machines to pick the cotton.

Haulers bring the picked cotton to a processing plant called a cotton gin. Machines dry the raw cotton fibers and remove any leaves or other trash. Another machine, called a gin stand, separates the cotton fibers, called lint, from the seeds. Then the lint is cleaned.

A bale press packs the cotton into 500-pound (227-kg) bales, wraps it with cloth, and binds it with steel bands. Trucks carry the refrigerator-sized bales to the warehouse. Then they are compressed, or squeezed, to about half their size to save space.

Government inspectors grade samples of the cotton. Growers then sell the graded cotton to brokers. Brokers, in turn, sell it to cloth manufacturers, who buy large amounts of cotton fiber for their textile plants.

When the cotton arrives at the textile plant, the bales are broken open, and machines clean the lint and roll it into a long sheet. Then spinning machines separate and straighten the cotton fibers. Other machines twist the fibers into fine, strong yarn.

Mechanical looms weave the yarn into cloth. Dyeing (coloring the cloth) and printing (stamping the cloth with patterns) finish the cloth.

_____ The cloth is dyed and printed.

_____ Mechanical looms weave the cotton yarn into cloth.

_____ Chemicals remove the leaves from the plants before picking.

_____ The cotton is packed into 500-pound (227-kg) bales.

_____ Cloth manufacturers buy cotton from brokers.

_____ Spinning machines separate and straighten the cotton fibers.

_____ At the cotton gin, the cotton lint is separated from the seeds.

_____ Cotton fibers are twisted into fine, strong yarn.

HOW TO IDENTIFY

Causes and their Effect

Apply Thinking Skills

DIRECTIONS: *Think about what you have read about the Southeast. For each effect, list two possible causes. Use the steps listed at the right to help you identify causes and effects.*

1. Identify the effect.

2. Look for all the causes of that effect.

3. Think about how the causes relate to each other and to the effect.

1. Effect: Many industries in the Southeast are related to agriculture.

Causes: **a.** _____

_____

_____

b. _____

_____

_____

2. Effect: Orlando, Florida, becomes a favorite place for tourists to go.

Causes: **a.** _____

_____

_____

b. _____

_____

_____

Harcourt Brace School Publishers

UNITED STATES PETROLEUM PRODUCTION

Make a Bar Graph

DIRECTIONS: Use the information in the table at the right to complete the bar graph below. In the blanks along the bottom of the graph, write the abbreviation for each state under the correct bar, starting at the left with the largest oil producer and ending at the right with the smallest. Label the left side of the graph to show what the numbers stand for.

STATE	PRODUCTION IN MILLIONS OF BARRELS
Alaska	627
California	305
Louisiana	143
Oklahoma	102
Texas	651
Wyoming	97

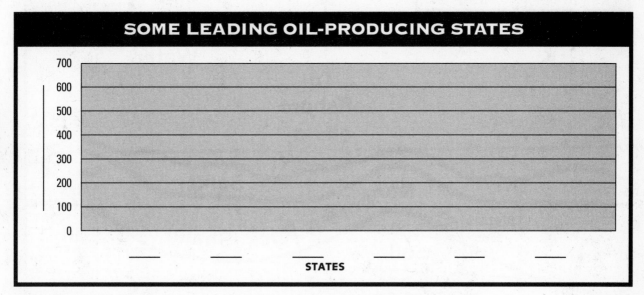

SOME LEADING OIL-PRODUCING STATES

STATES

DIRECTIONS: Use the information above to answer the following questions.

1. Where does Louisiana rank in United States oil production? _____

2. Which state is the nation's leading petroleum producer? _____

3. What is the advantage of presenting this information in a table?

_____

4. What is the advantage of presenting this information in a bar graph?

_____

HOW TO READ a Cross-Section Diagram

The drawing below is a cross-section diagram of the undersea petroleum fields that lie off the Gulf coast.

Apply Diagram Skills

DIRECTIONS: Study the cross-section diagram below. Then read the vocabulary key on page 45.

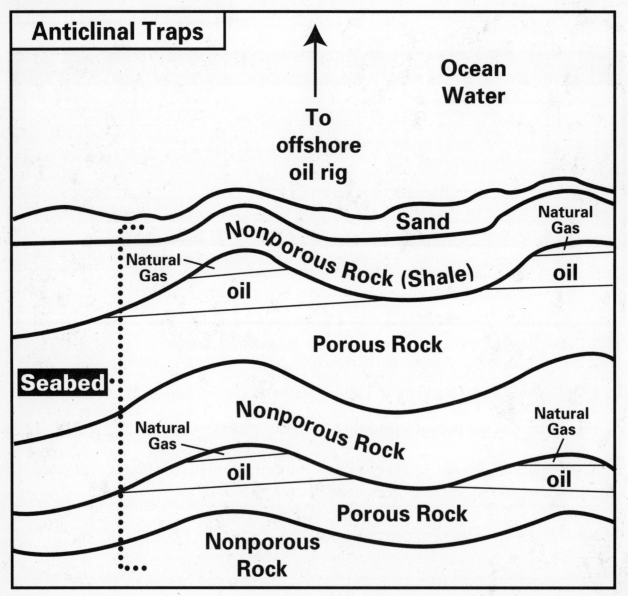

Anticlinal Traps

To offshore oil rig

Ocean Water

Sand

Natural Gas

Nonporous Rock (Shale)

Natural Gas

oil

oil

Porous Rock

Seabed

Nonporous Rock

Natural Gas

Natural Gas

oil

oil

Porous Rock

Nonporous Rock

(Continued)

Use after reading Chapter 6, Skill Lesson, pages 208–209.

VOCABULARY KEY

Porous rock has many small holes, or pores, that allow liquids, such as water or oil, to flow through it.

Nonporous rock will not let liquids pass through it.

Shale is nonporous rock made up of layers of compressed soil, clay, and minerals. Shale may contain some oil that seeped into the rock before it hardened.

A trap is an underground area where porous rock allows oil to pool or gather. Oil often is found in anticlinal, or dome-shaped, traps like the ones in the cross section.

DIRECTIONS: Use information from the cross-section diagram on page 44 and the vocabulary key to complete the following sentences.

1. The top layer of land under the ocean is _____.

2. Bubbles of _____ often form above the pools of oil.

3. _____ is a kind of nonporous rock that may contain oil.

4. The _____ is the name given to the layers of land under the ocean.

5. Oil can be found in dome-shaped traps called _____ traps.

DIRECTIONS: Follow these steps to complete the cross-section diagram on page 44.

1. Color the ocean water blue.

2. Color the layers of nonporous rock yellow.

3. Color the layers of porous rock brown.

4. Color the oil deposits red.

5. Color the natural gas deposits green.

6. Use a black crayon or marker to show the paths drill pipes should follow to reach the oil and gas resources in these anticlinal traps.

Harcourt Brace School Publishers

Use after reading Chapter 6, Skill Lesson, pages 208–209.

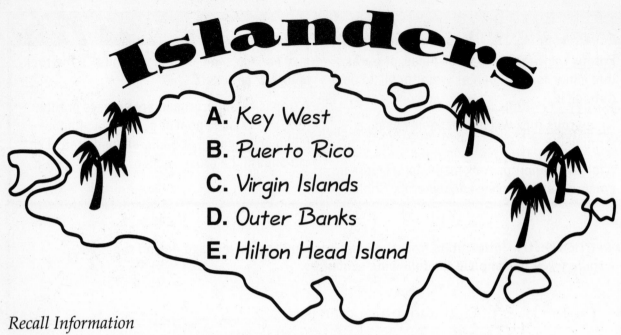

Islanders

A. Key West
B. Puerto Rico
C. Virgin Islands
D. Outer Banks
E. Hilton Head Island

Recall Information

DIRECTIONS: Read the descriptions from each islander below. Then match the description to the island or islands each person calls home. Write the correct letter on each line. Some letters may be used more than once.

____ **1.** "I spent time on these barrier islands with my pirate band. Legend says we buried our treasure there."

____ **2.** "My home is on one of these coral islands that lie along the north side of the Straits of Florida. I am connected to the mainland by more than 100 miles (160 km) of oceangoing highway."

____ **3.** "I live on St. Croix, one of three crowded islands that are part of this United States territory."

____ **4.** "I work at a hotel on this barrier island off the coast of South Carolina. This island is a popular vacation area."

____ **5.** "The language of my home island is Spanish, but I am an American citizen. Christopher Columbus landed here in 1493."

____ **6.** "My island was once connected to the mainland by a railroad, but a hurricane destroyed the tracks in 1935."

____ **7.** "My home is located in the tropics about 1,000 miles (1,609 km) southeast of Florida."

____ **8.** "The United States bought my islands from Denmark in 1917."

Use after reading Chapter 6, Lesson 4, pages 210–215.

NAME _____ DATE _____

COASTAL PLAINS AND *Islands*

Connect Main Ideas

DIRECTIONS: Use this organizer to show that you understand how the chapter's main ideas are connected. Complete the organizer by writing the main idea of each lesson.

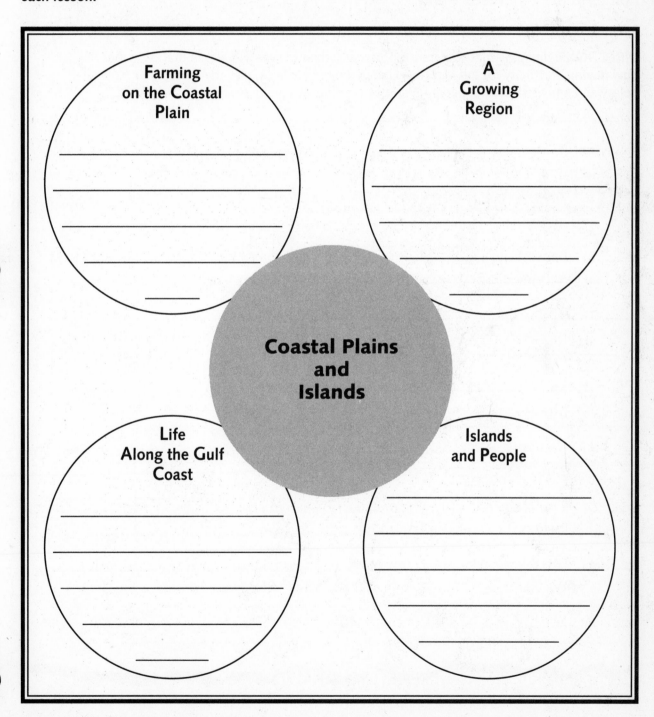

Farming
on the Coastal
Plain

_____

_____

_____

_____

A
Growing
Region

_____

_____

_____

_____

Coastal Plains
and
Islands

Life
Along the Gulf
Coast

_____

_____

_____

_____

Islands
and People

_____

_____

_____

_____

River Power

The Tennessee Valley Authority built dams to control flooding on the Tennessee River and its tributaries. The dams also provided electricity to thousands of farms and homes in the Tennessee Valley.

Write Creatively

DIRECTIONS: *Imagine that you are a reporter assigned to write an article that describes how having electricity for the first time changed people's lives. Use the newspaper page below and an extra sheet of paper if you need it. Illustrate your article with a drawing.*

Lights Go On in Tennessee Valley

by _____

_____

_____

_____

_____

_____

_____

_____

_____

_____

_____

_____

Harcourt Brace School Publishers

A CAPITAL
CITY

 Read a Street Map

DIRECTIONS:
Use the street map of downtown Atlanta, Georgia, to answer the questions below.

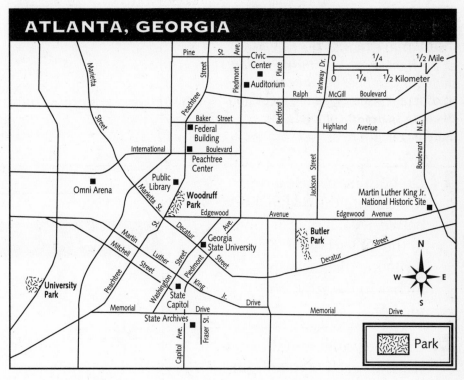

1. Atlanta is Georgia's capital. Which four streets surround the State

   Capitol building? _____

   _____

2. Which three streets surround the State Archives, a building where important

   government records are stored? _____

   _____

3. What state school is located at the corner of Decatur Street and Washington Street?

   _____

4. The federal government also has offices in Atlanta. The Federal Building sits at

   the corner of Peachtree Street and what other street? _____

HOW TO COMPARE
Distances on Maps

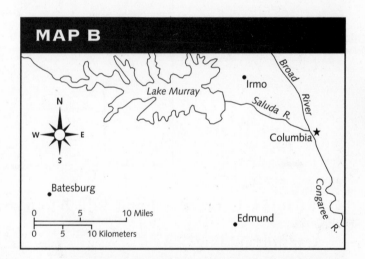

Apply Map Skills

DIRECTIONS: The two maps at the right both show the same part of South Carolina; but they are drawn at different scales. Use the maps and the map scales to complete the activities below.

1. On both maps, use a ruler to measure the distances between each pair of towns in the tables below. Then write the distances in inches in the table on the left.

2. Use your ruler and the map scale for each map to figure out how many miles the distances in inches stand for. Write your answers in the table on the right.

DISTANCE IN INCHES

DISTANCE BETWEEN	MAP A	MAP B
Columbia and Irmo		
Columbia and Batesburg		
Batesburg and Edmund		

DISTANCE IN MILES

DISTANCE BETWEEN	MAP A	MAP B
Columbia and Irmo		
Columbia and Batesburg		
Batesburg and Edmund		

Did you get the same distances between cities on both Map A and Map B? Why?

_____

Use after reading Chapter 7, Skill Lesson, pages 230–231.

Story Quilt

Generations of Appalachian quilt makers have passed on unique quilt patterns to their children. Some quilts are "story quilts." The designs of each square, the colors, and the materials used tell something about the quilt maker's family or home. For example, a certain quilt block may contain fabrics, or cloth, from the shirts or dresses that children wore on the first day of school, or from a favorite birthday dress.

The quilt maker sometimes needs to help younger family members understand the story. The quilt maker tells stories about the fabric and adds details from a memory. Sometimes the quilt maker uses fabrics to make pictures of familiar plants, animals, houses, and people. Some common quilt square patterns are shown below.

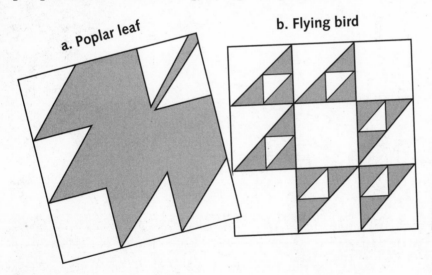

a. Poplar leaf b. Flying bird c. Bear paw

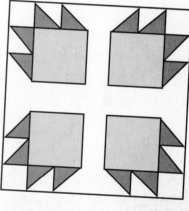

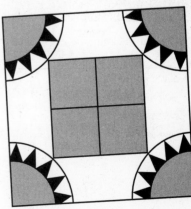

d. Sunflower

Respond with Art

DIRECTIONS: *Imagine you are a quilt maker. You want people to know about the region in which you live. On a separate sheet of paper, design a square for a story quilt that tells something about your part of the country.*

Harcourt Brace School Publishers

HOW TO UNDERSTAND Point of View

In 1775, Daniel Boone led a band of settlers along the Wilderness Road through the Cumberland Gap. The settlers, including Boone's wife and daughter, were on their way to Fort Boonesborough in Kentucky.

More than 75 years later, the artist George Caleb Bingham painted his idea of Boone's journey. The picture below is a drawing of Bingham's painting, *Daniel Boone Escorting Settlers Through the Cumberland Gap.*

Apply Thinking Skills

DIRECTIONS: Study the drawing. Then answer the questions on the next page.

(Continued)

Use after reading Chapter 7, Skill Lesson, page 236.

NAME _____ DATE _____

1. Can you tell which figure is meant to be Daniel Boone? How?

_____

_____

2. What does the drawing show you about the land near the Cumberland Gap?

_____

_____

_____

3. How do you think the artist feels about the pioneers? Explain your answer.

_____

_____

4. What useful things do the pioneers bring with them? _____

_____

_____

_____

5. Daniel Boone's expedition in September, 1775, included his wife and daughter. Why do you think the artist put the women in the center of the painting?

_____

_____

6. George Caleb Bingham was not yet born when Daniel Boone led his expedition. There were no cameras to take pictures. Bingham used his imagination to create his own vision of Boone's trip. What do you think Bingham hoped to say with

this picture? _____

_____

7. How does this picture make you feel? _____

_____

_____

Harcourt Brace School Publishers

Fire IN THE Mountain •

Read for Understanding

DIRECTIONS: Storytelling has a long tradition in Appalachia. Read this story, which is based on a Cherokee legend. Then complete the activity that follows.

Long, long ago, the People built a fire to burn the autumn leaves. The fire spread to a tree, and the tree burned to the ground. But the fire did not stop. It burned down into the roots of the tree. It made a great pit in the earth. No one knew what was feeding the fire, but it grew and grew.

The People worried. They looked into the hole, and it had no bottom. There was only a long, long dark tunnel, and at the end of the tunnel a fierce red light. Wherever the People walked, the earth felt hot.

"This fire will eat up our whole mountain!" the People thought. So they walked many days to the stream, filled many buckets, and poured the water down the hole. Clouds of steam came out, but the fire still burned.

"This fire is too big for us," the People said. "We'll call the Cold-Bringer from the North. He will bring the rain to put it out."

So Cold-Bringer came and shook his wet hair to make rain. The fire laughed and burned on. The angrier Cold-Bringer got, the colder it got. The People shivered, but the fire still burned. Cold-Bringer stamped his feet, shook his hair, and billows of snowflakes fell. But still the fire burned.

Finally, Cold-Bringer sent a great frozen shout into the hole. The hole filled up with ice. And it stayed that way for months! When the ice melted, there was no more fire in the earth, and the people had a beautiful blue bowl of water.

And the People say that sometimes, on an early spring night, you can still hear the crackling laughter of the fire under the ice.

DIRECTIONS: The story uses the language of legend to talk about common features of the Appalachian landscape. Unscramble the letters to find out what these are.

1. Fuel for the fire in the earth   aloc   _____

2. The bottomless pit   evac   _____

3. Cold-Bringer   wterni   _____

4. The blue bowl of water   keal   _____

5. The fire's crackling laughter   gripsn what   _____

      Use after reading Chapter 7, Lesson 4, pages 237–241.

Highlands and Mountains

Connect Main Ideas

DIRECTIONS: Use this organizer to show that you understand how the chapter's main ideas are connected. Complete the organizer by writing three examples for each main idea.

People in the Southeast have changed rivers to meet their needs.

1. _____

2. _____

3. _____

Rivers

Highlands and Mountains

The Piedmont   **Appalachia**

Many cities in the Piedmont have grown quickly.

1. _____

_____

2. _____

_____

3. _____

_____

People in Appalachia depend on their environment to earn a living.

1. _____

_____

2. _____

_____

3. _____

_____

Chasing a storm

Scientists who study tornadoes are sometimes called *storm chasers*. The story below is based on a magazine article about storm chasers.

Analyze a Magazine Story

DIRECTIONS: Read the passage below. Then answer the questions that follow.

As we drove within 10 miles of the storm, we saw the long, dark cloud base. Within minutes we spotted a twister shaped like an elephant's trunk. It hung from the rear of the main cloud tower.

Usually twisters move at a speed of about 30 miles per hour and last only a few minutes. But in that few minutes a twister can destroy everything in a path 150 feet wide. Some twisters, however, can be more than a mile wide, move at speeds of 60 miles per hour, and last for more than an hour.

Low on gas, we raced ahead of the twister as it moved directly at us. After a while, we stopped to watch the tornado. It had been on the ground for at least 14 miles. We saw it pass south of us and disappear into the darkness.

1. What is another name for a tornado? _____

2. How did the writer describe the shape of the tornado? _____

_____

3. On a separate sheet of paper, draw a picture of the description given in the first paragraph.

4. How wide is the damage path of most tornadoes? _____

5. Imagine you are a storm chaser. On a separate sheet of paper, write a note to a friend telling what it is like to see a tornado up close.

Harcourt Brace School Publishers

Use after reading Chapter 8, Lesson 1, pages 259–263.

HOW TO READ Pictographs

Apply Graph Skills

DIRECTIONS: Use the information in the pictograph to answer the questions below. Write your answers on a separate sheet of paper.

CORN PRODUCTION		
STATE	**1992**	**1993**
Illinois	🌽🌽🌽🌽🌽🌽🌽🌽🌽🌽🌽🌽🌽🌽🌽	🌽🌽🌽🌽🌽🌽🌽🌽🌽🌽🌽🌽🌽🌽
Iowa	🌽🌽🌽🌽🌽🌽🌽🌽🌽🌽🌽🌽🌽🌽🌽🌽🌽🌽	🌽🌽🌽🌽🌽🌽🌽🌽🌽
Kansas	🌽🌽🌽	🌽🌽
South Dakota	🌽🌽🌽	🌽🌽
🌽 = 100 MILLION BUSHELS		

1. Which state in the pictograph produced the most corn in 1992?

2. Which state in the pictograph produced the most corn in 1993?

3. How much more corn did Kansas produce in 1992 than in 1993?

4. Which state's corn production dropped the most from 1992 to 1993?

5. Which of the two years shown in the pictograph had higher levels of corn production?

6. What do you think might have been responsible for the smaller corn crops of 1993?

Life in a Soddy

Identify Items from Different Time Periods

DIRECTIONS: Use what you know about life in a sod house in 1875, as well as your own common sense, to decide which items do not belong in the picture. Circle the things that are out of place. Then, on the lines below, tell which circled item you would find it most difficult to live without. Explain your answer.

_____

_____

_____

_____

Use after reading Chapter 8, Lesson 2, pages 265–269.

HOW TO IDENTIFY
TIME PATTERNS

The list below shows some important tasks that a wheat farmer might follow to try to ensure a successful crop. The tasks are listed in the order in which the farmer performs them.

Apply Reading and Writing Skills

DIRECTIONS: *Write a short article describing the steps wheat farmers might follow. Use words like* first, second, then, *and* finally *to describe the order of steps in a farmer's work.*

Tasks of a Wheat Farmer

1. Plowing

2. Planting the seeds

3. Cultivating (breaking up the soil around new plants to allow the roots to get air and water)

4. Weeding (removing weeds by hand, by machine, or with chemicals)

5. Fertilizing

6. Irrigating (adding water to dry soil)

7. Reaping (harvesting the ripe grain)

8. Threshing (separating the grain from the rest of the plant)

_____

_____

_____

_____

_____

_____

DIRECTIONS: *Exchange your article with a classmate. Circle all the words in your classmate's article that show time patterns.*

Use after reading Chapter 8, Skill Lesson, page 270.

Harcourt Brace School Publishers

NAME _____ DATE _____

THE RAILROAD

Recall Facts

DIRECTIONS: Supply the missing word or words each sentence needs.
Hint: Unload the words you need from the railroad cars.

Chisholm demand	flour Topeka	iron cereals	Omaha supply
meat packing	Great Plains	Dakota lead	free enterprise

1. On the _____ , railroad tracks usually followed rivers because the steam engines that pulled the trains needed water. Cities that grew along these

    railroad tracks include _____ , Nebraska, and _____ , Kansas.

2. The most famous cattle trail was called the _____ Trail.

3. The raising of cattle has made _____ a leading business in several states.

4. Minnesota has one of the largest _____ ore deposits in the world,

    South _____ has the largest gold mine in the country, and

    Missouri is an important producer of _____ .

5. To save shipping costs, _____ mills are located in several cities in the

    Middle West. In other cities workers use corn and wheat to make _____ .

6. The United States has a _____ economy, in which the _____

    of goods and services usually rises when the _____ is great.

Use after reading Chapter 8, Lesson 3, pages 271–275.

Harcourt Brace School Publishers

HOW TO FOLLOW ROUTES on a ROAD MAP

 Apply Map Skills

DIRECTIONS: Use this road map of Nebraska to describe the route outlined below.

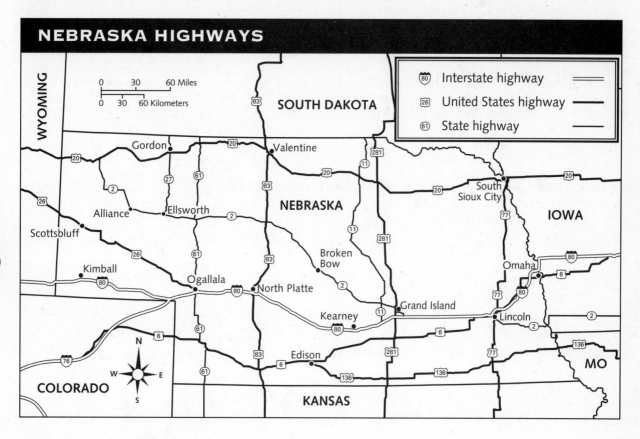

Describe the best route that would . . .

1. begin in Alliance and take a state highway to Grand Island for the Husker Harvest Days celebration.

_____

2. take you from Grand Island to the National Roller Skating Museum in Lincoln.

_____

3. take you from Lincoln to South Sioux City.

_____

PAMPA or PLAINS?

Summarize a Lesson

DIRECTIONS: Identify whether each of the statements below applies to the Pampa of Argentina, the Interior Plains of the United States, or both regions.

1. The western half is much drier than the eastern half. _____

2. The growing season is from December to March. _____

3. The Mississippi River flows here. _____

4. Settlers on the prairie often built sod houses. _____

5. Ranches called estancias cover thousands of acres. _____

6. The Andes Mountains form the western border. _____

7. Corn grows well in the eastern half. _____

8. The western part is sometimes called the Nation's Breadbasket. _____

9. Meat packing is an important industry. _____

10. Ranch hands are known as gauchos. _____

DIRECTIONS: On the lines below, write one additional statement describing the Pampa, one describing the Interior Plains, and one describing both regions.

The Pampa _____

_____

The Interior Plains _____

_____

Both _____

_____

Harcourt Brace School Publishers

Use after reading Chapter 8, Lesson 4, pages 278–281.

NAME _____ DATE _____

THE INTERIOR PLAINS

Connect Main Ideas

DIRECTIONS: Use this organizer to show that you understand how the chapter's main ideas are connected. Complete the organizer by writing two sentences about each main idea.

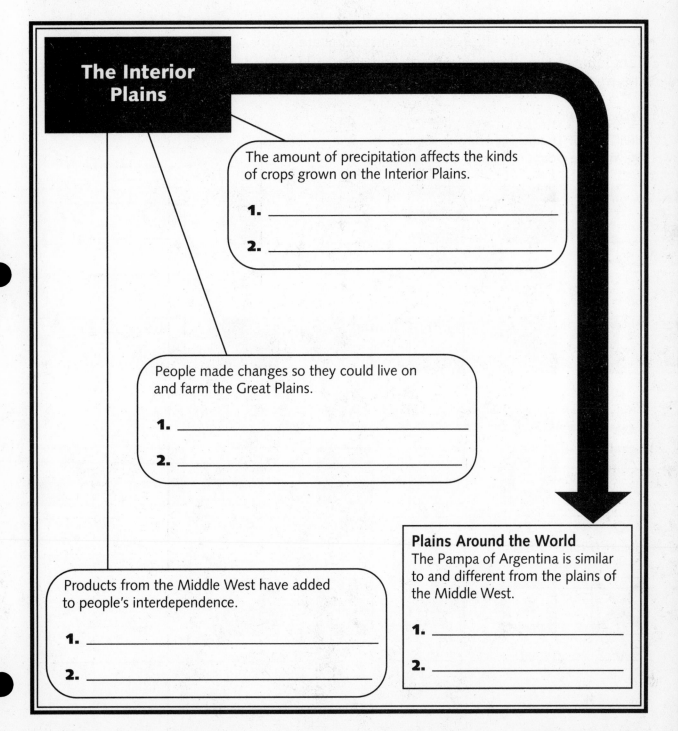

The Interior Plains

The amount of precipitation affects the kinds of crops grown on the Interior Plains.

1. _____

2. _____

People made changes so they could live on and farm the Great Plains.

1. _____

2. _____

Products from the Middle West have added to people's interdependence.

1. _____

2. _____

Plains Around the World
The Pampa of Argentina is similar to and different from the plains of the Middle West.

1. _____

2. _____

Harcourt Brace School Publishers

Use after reading Chapter 8, pages 258–281.

GREAT LAKES SIGNALS

Each year, hundreds upon hundreds of ships visit the Great Lakes ports. When crews from different ships want to communicate with each other, they often raise signal flags to spell out short messages. Each flag stands for a letter of the alphabet. There also are flags for numbers.

Decode Symbols

DIRECTIONS: Use the key below to help you decode the messages shown by the groups of flags on the next page.

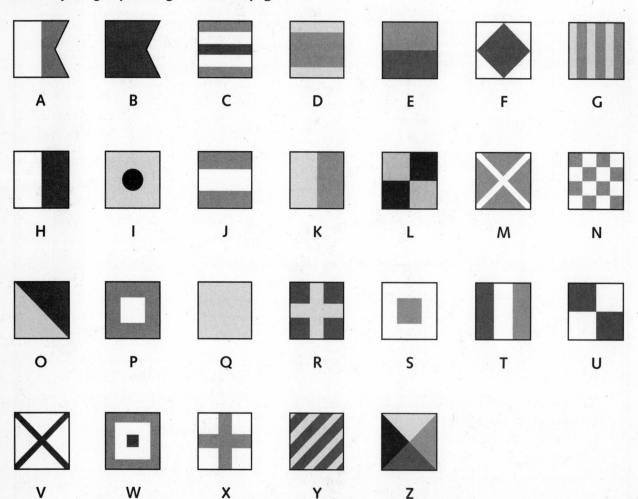

(Continued)

Use after reading Chapter 9, Lesson 1, pages 285–289.

NAME _____ DATE _____

DIRECTIONS: Use the code key to read each "signal" below. Write the correct word or group of words on the line below the signal.

1. _____

2. _____

3. _____

4. _____

5. _____

DIRECTIONS: Match each word or group of words above with its description below. Write the number of the word or group of words on the correct line.

_____ **a.** Connects Lake Michigan and the Illinois River

_____ **b.** Industry that gave birth to the city of Gary, Indiana

_____ **c.** Line of workers along which a product moves as it is put together one step at a time

_____ **d.** Resources that include money, buildings, machines, and tools

_____ **e.** Michigan city where the United States automobile industry began

Around the
RIVER BEND

This map of the Middle West in 1870 shows the Dakota Territory, which later became the states of North Dakota and South Dakota. The map also shows some of the towns and cities that grew up along rivers in the Middle West. These rivers provided people with important transportation and trade routes.

Understand the Importance of Rivers

DIRECTIONS: Study the map. Then answer the questions that follow.

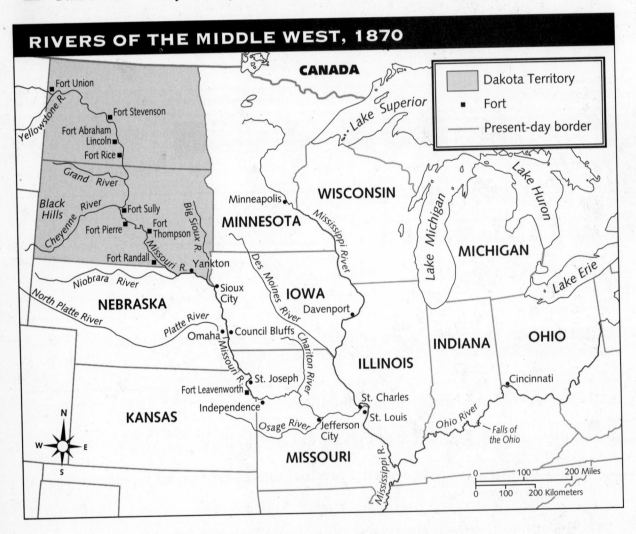

1. Which fort in the Dakota Territory is located where the Cheyenne River flows

   into the Missouri River? _____

   (Continued)

Use after reading Chapter 9, Lesson 2, pages 290–294.

2. Imagine you are traveling by river in 1870. According to the map, which river or rivers could you use if you were going from

   a. Cincinnati, Ohio, to St. Louis, Missouri?

   _____

   b. Fort Leavenworth, Kansas, to Sioux City, Iowa?

   _____

   c. Council Bluffs, Iowa, to the Black Hills in the Dakota Territory?

   _____

3. Which river begins in Kansas and flows east to join the Missouri River near Jefferson City, Missouri?

   _____

4. Which river forms part of the border between Iowa and Missouri?

   _____

5. Which fort in the Dakota Territory is farthest north?

   _____

   Near which two rivers is it located?

   _____

6. Into what large river does the Platte River flow?

   _____

DIRECTIONS: By 1870 most river travel was done by steamboat. Before steamboats were used, however, people mostly traveled by flatboat or keelboat. On a separate sheet of paper, draw a scene of people traveling by flatboat, keelboat, or steamboat. Write a caption for your drawing. Tell why you chose to draw the type of boat you did.

Harcourt Brace School Publishers

River Poems

Here are three examples of poems that have been written to describe some of the great rivers of the world.

Connect Geography and Literature

The Nile

All day long, day after day,
We follow the sacred body of the river,
All that is above us is below us—
Blueness and space and the brightness of the sun,
We scatter the clouds rippling in our wake by day.
We look down upon the stars by night.
       —from "The Nile" by Elizabeth Coatsworth

The Chang Jiang

Climbing the tower, I gaze absently
    down on boats that come and go. . . .
. . . spellbound by the color of the grasses,
    I sit by the water's edge.
Nothing but spring river, and I never
    tire of watching it—
rounding the sand spits, circling rocks,
    a rippling, murmuring green.
         —from "Spring River" by Po Chü-i

The Mississippi

And the river waits.
The river listens,
Chuckling little banjo-notes that break with a flop on the stillness;
And by the low dark shed that holds the heavy freights,
Two lonely cypress trees stand up and point with stiffened fingers
Far southward where a single chimney stands out aloof in the sky.
       —from "Down the Mississippi" by John Gould Fletcher

DIRECTIONS: On a separate sheet of paper, write a short poem about a river you have studied, visited, or imagined. Use descriptive language.

Harcourt Brace School Publishers

HOW TO USE A TABLE TO GROUP Information

Apply Chart and Graph Skills

DIRECTIONS: Use the following information to complete the tables below.

You have learned to classify information in different ways. For example, you can classify rivers by their length or by continent. Here is some information about five of the world's great rivers:

- The Nile flows through Burundi, Uganda, Sudan, and Egypt. Its drainage basin covers 1,293,000 square miles (3,349,000 sq km).
- The Mississippi flows through the United States. Its drainage basin covers 1,247,300 square miles (3,230,490 sq km).
- The Amazon flows through Peru, Venezuela, Ecuador, Colombia, Bolivia, and Brazil. Its drainage basin covers 2,700,000 square miles (7,000,000 sq km).
- The Ganges flows through India and Bangladesh. Its drainage basin covers 376,800 square miles (975,900 sq km).
- The Chang Jiang flows through China. Its drainage basin covers 706,000 square miles (1,829,000 sq km).

A. To complete Table A, list the rivers in order by size of drainage basin.

B. To complete Table B, list the rivers in alphabetical order.

C. To complete Table C, list the rivers in order of the number of countries through which they pass.

A	B	C

Gifts of the Rain Forest

These are some of the products and resources that come from rain forests.

BANANAS	COCONUTS	RUBBER
CASHEWS	FERNS	SWEET POTATOES
CHEWING GUM	MEDICINES	TEA
CHOCOLATE	PAPAYAS	VANILLA
COCOA	PINEAPPLES	VEGETABLE OILS

Develop Social Studies Vocabulary

DIRECTIONS: Find each of the rain forest products and resources in the word-search grid below. The words are printed from top to bottom. Color in the squares that make up each of the words you find.

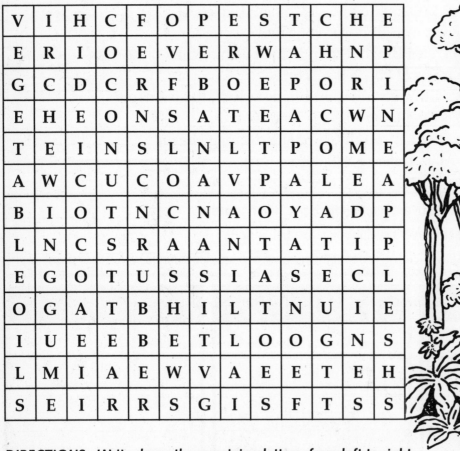

V	I	H	C	F	O	P	E	S	T	C	H	E
E	R	I	O	E	V	E	R	W	A	H	N	P
G	C	D	C	R	F	B	O	E	P	O	R	I
E	H	E	O	N	S	A	T	E	A	C	W	N
T	E	I	N	S	L	N	L	T	P	O	M	E
A	W	C	U	O	A	V	P	A	L	E	A	
B	I	O	T	N	C	N	A	O	Y	A	D	P
L	N	C	S	R	A	A	N	T	A	T	I	P
E	G	O	T	U	S	S	I	A	S	E	C	L
O	G	A	T	B	H	I	L	T	N	U	I	E
I	U	E	E	B	E	T	L	O	O	G	N	S
L	M	I	A	E	W	V	A	E	E	T	E	H
S	E	I	R	R	S	G	I	S	F	T	S	S

DIRECTIONS: Write down the remaining letters, from left to right, in the space below. Then read what Paulo's father wishes.

_____

Use after reading Chapter 9, Lesson 4, pages 301–305.

Harcourt Brace School Publishers

• GREAT WATERWAYS
Shape Nations

Connect Main Ideas

DIRECTIONS: Use this organizer to show that you understand how the chapter's main ideas are connected. Complete the organizer by writing details about the main ideas and about each river.

Great Waterways Shape Nations

Along the Great Lakes
Many large cities and industries have grown up along the Great Lakes.

_____

_____

River Transportation
The Mississippi River system has been used for transportation and trade routes.

_____

_____

The Nile River

_____

_____

Rivers Around the World
People in different places use rivers in different ways.

The Amazon River

_____

_____

The Rhine River

_____

_____

The Chang Jiang

_____

_____

The Ganges River

_____

_____

SOUTHWEST LANDFORMS

Identify Landform Regions on a Map

DIRECTIONS: Use the map below to answer the questions that follow.

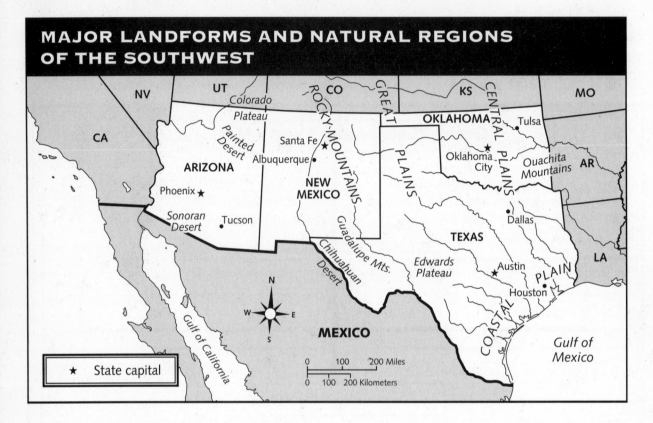

MAJOR LANDFORMS AND NATURAL REGIONS OF THE SOUTHWEST

★ State capital

1. Which landform covers the northeastern corner of Arizona? _____

2. In which natural region is Oklahoma City located? _____

3. In which natural region is Houston located? _____

4. Which city is shown at the edge of the Rocky Mountains?

_____

5. Which state is most likely to have the most agricultural activity? Why?

_____

6. What desert is located near Tucson? _____

Use after reading Chapter 10, Lesson 1, pages 323–329.

Naming *the Land*

The names of many towns, cities, and physical features in the Southwest reflect the Indian and Spanish heritage of this region.

Recognize Cultural Heritage

DIRECTIONS: Use the information in the table below to answer the questions that follow.

PLACE NAME	LANGUAGE	MEANING
Amarillo, TX	Spanish	"Yellow"—named for the color of the rocks and soil
Cimarron River, OK	Spanish	"Wild, untamed"
Harcuvar Peak, AZ	Mojave Indian	"There is very little water here."
Sandia Mountains, NM	Spanish	"Watermelon"—named for the mountains' pink color at sunset
Tucumcari, NM	Comanche Indian	"Lookout place"
Tulsa, OK	Muskogee Indian	"Our town"

1. Which place name describes the desert? _____

_____

2. Which place names refer to the color of the land? _____

_____

3. Do you think the first settlers saw the Cimarron River as slow-moving and

calm or as rapid and rough? Why? _____

_____

4. Do you think there is high ground at Tucumcari? Why or why not?

_____

_____

HOW TO READ A VERTICAL TIME LINE

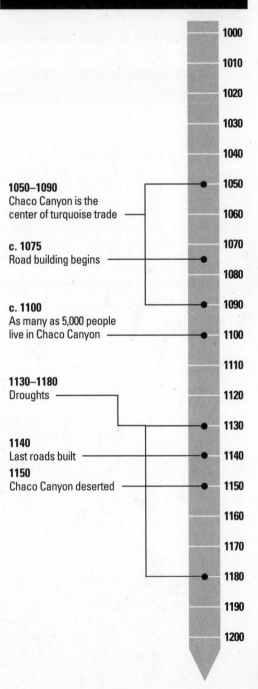

CHACO CANYON CULTURE

One place where the Anasazi built settlements was beneath the towering rock walls of Chaco (CHAH•koh) Canyon, in what is today New Mexico.

Apply Time Line Skills

DIRECTIONS: Use the time line at the right to answer the questions below. The c. before a date stands for circa, which means "around." The c. is used when historians do not have an exact date.

1. When did the Anasazi people begin building the Chaco Canyon roads?

   _____

2. What was the last year in which Chaco Canyon roads were built?

   _____

3. In what year did as many as 5,000 people live in the Chaco Canyon community?

   _____

4. When did the droughts begin in Chaco

   Canyon? _____

5. How many decades did the droughts last?

   _____

6. By what year had the Anasazi people left

   Chaco Canyon? _____

Time line labels:

1050–1090
Chaco Canyon is the center of turquoise trade

c. 1075
Road building begins

c. 1100
As many as 5,000 people live in Chaco Canyon

1130–1180
Droughts

1140
Last roads built

1150
Chaco Canyon deserted

1000 1010 1020 1030 1040 1050 1060 1070 1080 1090 1100 1110 1120 1130 1140 1150 1160 1170 1180 1190 1200

Harcourt Brace School Publishers

The Growing SOUTHWEST

Use Graphs to Find Information

DIRECTIONS: Use the graphs below to answer the questions that follow.

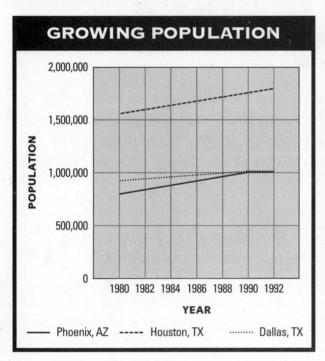

GROWING POPULATION

POPULATION

2,000,000

1,500,000

1,000,000

500,000

0

1980 1982 1984 1986 1988 1990 1992

YEAR

—— Phoenix, AZ ----- Houston, TX ········ Dallas, TX

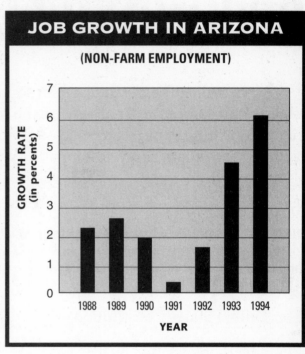

JOB GROWTH IN ARIZONA

(NON-FARM EMPLOYMENT)

GROWTH RATE (in percents)

7
6
5
4
3
2
1
0

1988 1989 1990 1991 1992 1993 1994

YEAR

1. Which city had more than one million people in 1980? _____

2. Which city's population grew the least between 1980 and 1990?

_____

3. Which two cities had similar population numbers in 1992?

_____

4. In which year did Arizona have the highest rate of job growth?

_____

5. In which year did Arizona have the lowest rate of job growth?

_____

HOW TO TELL PRIMARY FROM SECONDARY SOURCES

A primary source is made when someone who saw or took part in an event records it in some way. That way can be in writing, such as in a letter or a document of the time. It also can be through sculpture or videotape or audiotape or pictures. Secondary sources are made by people who are relating what someone else saw or did.

Apply Thinking Skills

DIRECTIONS: Decide whether each of the items below is a primary or a secondary source. Then place a P for Primary or an S for Secondary to the left of each statement. On a separate sheet of paper, explain your answers.

_____ United States Constitution

_____ a textbook written in 1861

_____ an encyclopedia article about computers

_____ a story written about a baseball game, based on the author's interview of people who saw the game

_____ a soldier's diary describing a battle in which the soldier took part

_____ an audio recording of someone describing a fire she helped to put out

_____ a photograph of a crime scene

Harcourt Brace School Publishers

Use after reading Chapter 10, Skill Lesson, page 340.

NAME _____ DATE _____

Working Together to
SAVE A RIVER

Think Creatively

DIRECTIONS: *Think of a way that fourth graders from the United States and fourth graders from Mexico could work together to improve the Rio Grande's environment. Then fill out the Project Description Form below.*

Project Description Form

1. What is your project called? _____

_____

2. How will your project help the environment of the Rio Grande area?

_____

_____

3. How will you help fourth graders from the United States and fourth graders

from Mexico work together? _____

_____

4. In the Before box below draw a picture of the Rio Grande area today. In the After box draw a picture showing what the Rio Grande area might look like after your project is completed.

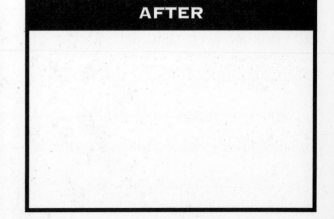

BEFORE	**AFTER**

HOW TO RESOLVE CONFLICT BY COMPROMISE

Imagine that your city or town has passed a law against skateboarding on sidewalks or in playgrounds. As a result, some skateboarders have started skating in dangerous places, such as parking lots or drainage tunnels. Many skateboarders feel that the law is unfair.

Apply Thinking Skills

DIRECTIONS: Use the process you learned in your textbook to help work out a compromise for this conflict. Write your answers on the lines below. Then compare your ideas for a compromise with those of a partner.

1. Identify what is causing the conflict.

_____

_____

2. State what each side wants.

_____

_____

3. Decide what each side wants most and what each side is willing to give up.

_____

_____

4. Look for ways that each side can get most of what it wants.

_____

_____

5. Take steps to see that the compromise will work over time.

_____

_____

Use after reading Chapter 10, Skill Lesson, page 345.

Harcourt Brace School Publishers

A Changing Landscape

Connect Main Ideas

DIRECTIONS: Use this organizer to show that you understand how the chapter's main ideas are connected. Complete the organizer by writing a sentence or two to summarize the main idea of each lesson.

A Changing Landscape

The Land and its Resources

_____

_____

_____

_____

Sharing a River

_____

_____

_____

_____

The Southwest Long Ago

_____

_____

_____

_____

A Changing Region

_____

_____

_____

_____

Use after reading Chapter 10, pages 322–347.

WATER IN THE DESERT

Solve a Word Puzzle

DIRECTIONS: Use the clues below to solve the crossword puzzle on the next page.

Across

1. This is one of the world's largest reservoirs. It holds the waters of the Colorado River. (2 words)
5. The valleys of the Salt River and the _____ _____ were the first parts of the Arizona desert to be settled. (2 words)
6. A deep, water-carved gully or ditch
7. The name of the desert that covers most of southwest Arizona
9. A sudden, heavy rain
10. A person who has no permanent home but keeps moving from place to place
11. Most places in the desert receive _____ only a few times a year.

Down

2. Someone who moves from farm to farm with the seasons, harvesting crops (2 words)
3. Wells use modern technology to pump this kind of water from deep beneath the Earth's surface.
4. The _____ Arizona Project was built to bring water to desert cities.
6. A large pipe or canal built to carry water
8. Indians of this culture came to the Sonoran Desert about 2,000 years ago.

DIRECTIONS: After completing the crossword puzzle, copy on the lines below the letters that appear in the heavily outlined boxes.

_____ _____ _____ _____ _____ _____ _____ _____ _____ _____

DIRECTIONS: Now unscramble the letters to answer this riddle.

What is 660 feet (201 m) thick at its base, contains enough concrete to pave a two-land highway from New York City to San Francisco, and is shown in the drawing on the next page?

_____ _____ _____ _____ _____ _____ _____ _____ _____ _____

(Continued)

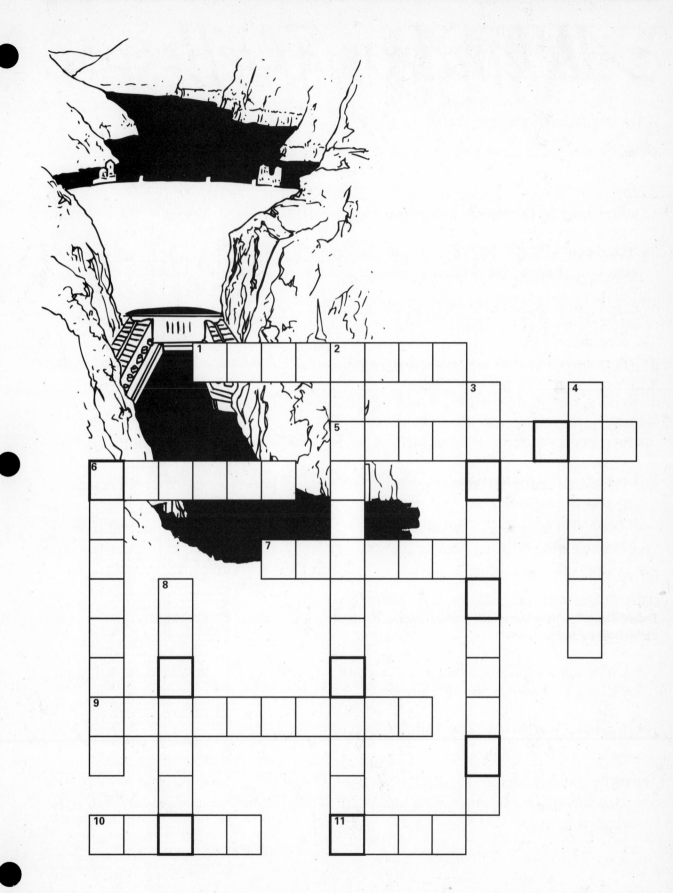

Alejandro's Well

How a Windmill Pumps Water

1. The tail vane steers the propeller blades toward the wind.

2. Wind catches the blades and turns the wheel.

3. Small gears on the wheel shaft turn larger gears, increasing the power.

4. Connecting rods on the large gears move the pump rod up and down.

5. The pump rod connects to the pump handle.

6. Raising the pump handle pushes the piston down and opens the valve. Water enters the pipe.

7. Lowering the pump handle pulls the piston up and closes the valve. Water in the pipe is forced upward by pressure each time the handle is lowered.

Interpret a Cross-Section Diagram

DIRECTIONS: After examining the cross-section diagram and reading "How a Windmill Pumps Water," complete the activities below.

- Color the water blue, the stones and soil yellow, and the brick well lining red.

- Add black arrows to show the motion of the pump handle and the piston.

- On a separate sheet of paper, use your own words to describe how a windmill pumps water.

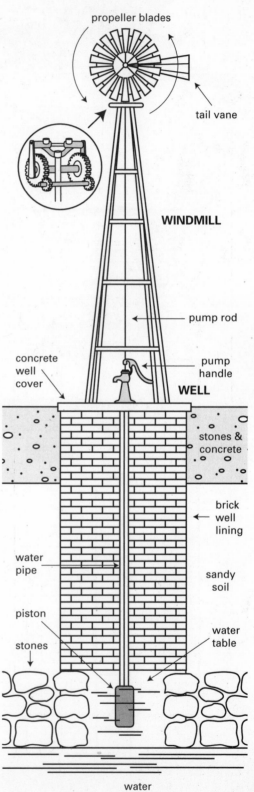

propeller blades

tail vane

WINDMILL

pump rod

concrete well cover

pump handle

WELL

stones & concrete

brick well lining

water pipe

sandy soil

piston

stones

water table

water

Harcourt Brace School Publishers

Use after reading Chapter 11, Lesson 2, pages 356–360.

Tucson City Government

Read an Organizational Chart

DIRECTIONS: The chart below shows how the government of the city of Tucson, Arizona, is organized. Use this chart to answer the questions that follow.

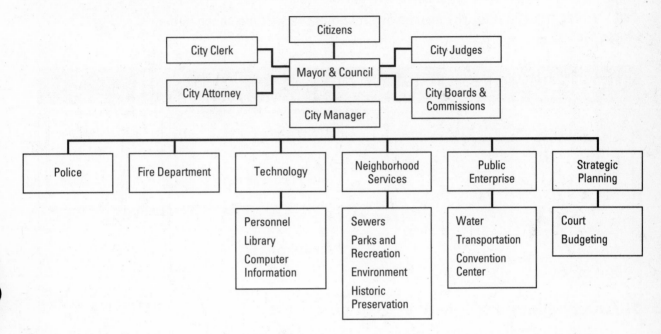

1. To whom are the mayor and council responsible? _____

2. To whom is the city clerk directly responsible? _____

3. According to this chart, who is responsible for the day-to-day operations

   of the city? _____

4. Which city department provides water to the people of Tucson?

   _____

5. If the mayor or a member of the council wanted to speak to someone in the

   police department, whom should he or she talk to first? Why? _____

   _____

   _____

Use after reading Chapter 11, Lesson 3, pages 361–365.

HOW TO USE A TIME ZONE MAP

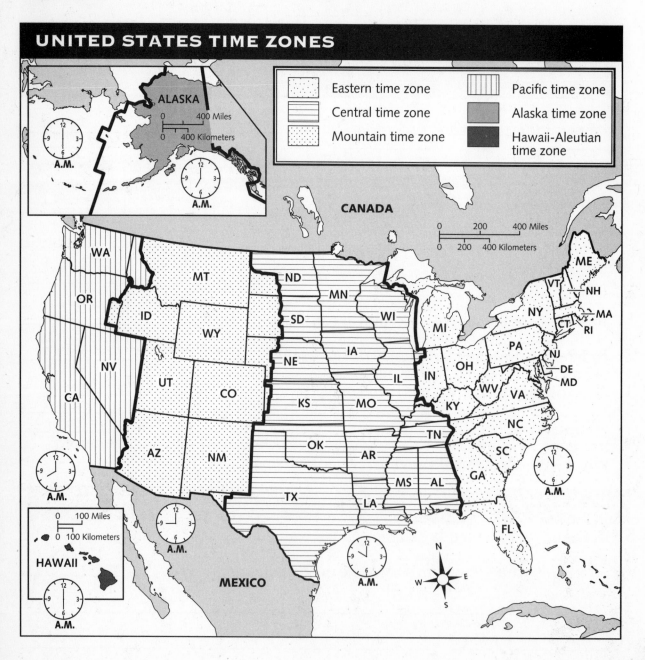

Apply Map Skills

DIRECTIONS: Study the map below. It shows the six time zones in the United States.

UNITED STATES TIME ZONES

Legend:
- Eastern time zone
- Central time zone
- Mountain time zone
- Pacific time zone
- Alaska time zone
- Hawaii-Aleutian time zone

ALASKA

HAWAII

CANADA

MEXICO

(Continued)

DIRECTIONS: *Label your town or city on the map.*
Then use the map to answer the questions.

1. In which time zone do you live? _____

2. When it is 4:00 P.M. in the afternoon in New Mexico, what time
is it in . . .

- Maine? _____

- California? _____

- Hawaii? _____

- Minnesota? _____

- Colorado? _____

3. Some states fall in two different time zones. That means people in neighboring
towns might set their clocks differently! Study the map. Then list five states that
have more than one time zone.

_____

_____

_____

4. Many offices close at 5:00 P.M. If you live in Washington State and you want to
call an office in New York, when is the latest time you should call?

_____

5. It is noon in Missouri. Draw hands on the clocks below, showing the correct
time for each state.

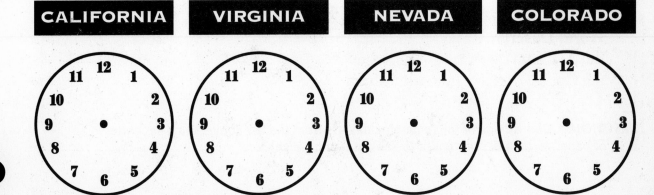

| CALIFORNIA | VIRGINIA | NEVADA | COLORADO |

Desert Portraits

Recall Information Through Art and Writing

DIRECTIONS: Study the picture and read the description below it. Then select from the list of four deserts the name of the one that you think is pictured. Write its name on the line.

I have very little sand.
I am cold for much of the year.
My soil is rocky.
I lie on a high plateau in central Asia.
Most of my people are wandering herders of cattle, goats, and sheep.
My plant life is limited to desert grass and small shrubs.
Wild horses, gazelles, and antelope roam here.

I am the _____ .

World Deserts

the Atacama   the Negev
the Gobi   the Sahara

DIRECTIONS: Choose one of the remaining deserts from the list above. On a separate sheet of paper, write a description of the desert you have chosen.

Harcourt Brace School Publishers

A Land of Deserts

Connect Main Ideas

DIRECTIONS: Use this organizer to show that you understand how the chapter's main ideas are connected. Complete each box by writing three details about each main idea.

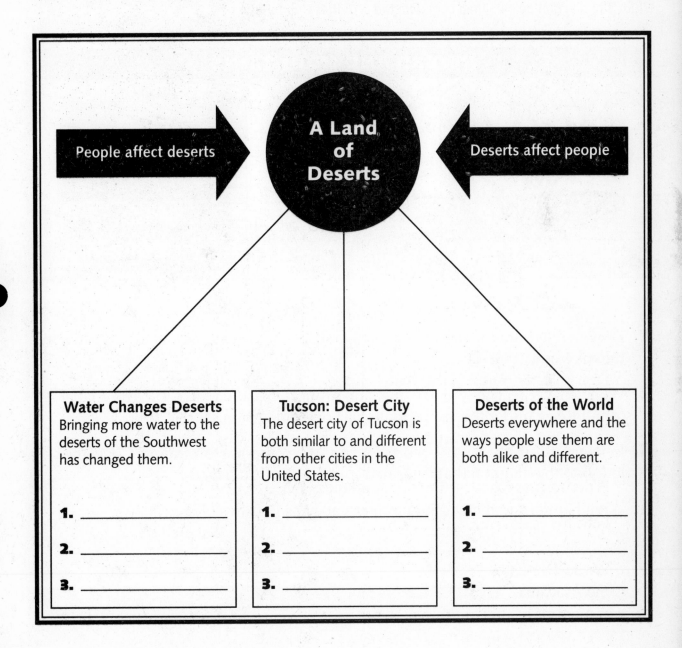

People affect deserts → **A Land of Deserts** ← Deserts affect people

Water Changes Deserts
Bringing more water to the deserts of the Southwest has changed them.

1. _____
2. _____
3. _____

Tucson: Desert City
The desert city of Tucson is both similar to and different from other cities in the United States.

1. _____
2. _____
3. _____

Deserts of the World
Deserts everywhere and the ways people use them are both alike and different.

1. _____
2. _____
3. _____

Use after reading Chapter 11, pages 348–373.

Rivers & Mountains

Analyze a Diagram

DIRECTIONS: Rivers play a very important role in the erosion of hills and mountains. Study the diagram below. Then complete the activities that follow.

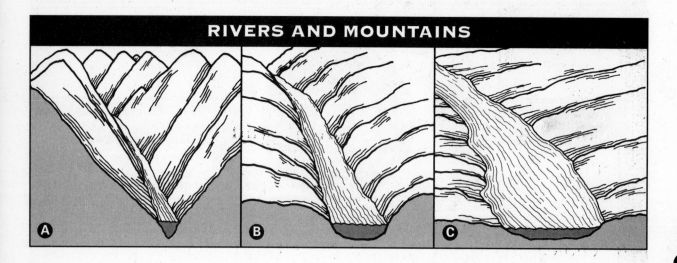

RIVERS AND MOUNTAINS

A   B   C

1. Draw a line from the highest point of land to the lowest point of land shown in the diagram.

2. When a river reaches old age, the land around it is at its lowest. Write a label for Old Age under the appropriate part of the diagram.

3. In its youthful stage, a river forms a very steep and narrow valley. Circle the letter on the diagram that is located under a youthful river.

4. What happens to the width of a river valley as it grows older?

_____

_____

5. At which stage do you think a river's power of erosion is the greatest? Why?

_____

_____

Use after reading Chapter 12, Lesson 1, pages 387–391.

Transcontinental Railroad

Analyze Points of View

DIRECTIONS: Each of the four paragraphs below reflects an opinion about the building of the transcontinental railroad. Read the paragraphs. Then answer the questions that follow.

Paragraph A
The transcontinental railroad will bring us together as a country. It will open up new lands. It will make everyone rich—the railroad owners, the merchants who sell goods in the West, and the workers who will build the railroad and the towns along its route.

Paragraph B
The railroad will destroy our people. As the railroads cross the plains, hunters will kill the buffalo. Our people depend on the buffalo for food. We use its skin for clothing and shelter. How will we live when the buffalo is gone?

Paragraph C
Why do we need a transcontinental railroad to connect us to the West? After all, canalers and shipping companies do a fine job of supplying Eastern needs. This railroad could hurt my business.

Paragraph D
We need the railroad. Where else can immigrants find jobs? No one else will hire us. We don't make much money working on the railroad, and the work is hard and dangerous. But it is better than nothing.

1. Which paragraphs contain opinions in favor of building the railroad? _____

2. Which paragraphs contain opinions opposed to building the railroad? _____

3. Match each of the people below with the paragraph above that might best reflect his or her opinion:

a Chinese immigrant _____   a New York canaler _____

a San Francisco banker _____   a Cheyenne chief _____

4. If you lived at the time of the building of the transcontinental railroad, which of these opinions do you think you would share? Why? Use a separate sheet of paper to answer this question.

HOW TO USE A Road Map and a Mileage Table

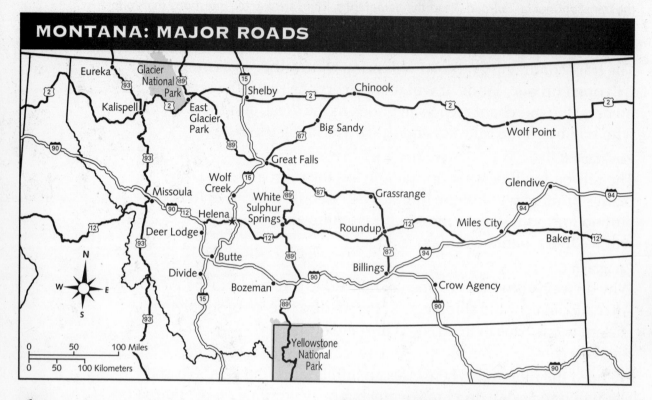

MONTANA: MAJOR ROADS

Apply Map Skills

DIRECTIONS: Use the mileage table to determine the distance for each of the following trips. Then trace each trip on the road map in the color suggested.

	Billings	Butte	Glendive	Great Falls	Kalispell
Billings		236	221	224	452
Butte	236		457	157	240
Glendive	221	457		353	581
Great Falls	224	157	353		228
Kalispell	452	240	581	228	

		Distance	Color
1.	Kalispell to Butte	_____	Red
2.	Great Falls to Butte	_____	Green
3.	Billings to Glendive	_____	Purple
4.	Kalispell to Great Falls	_____	Blue

Use after reading Chapter 12, Skill Lesson, pages 396–397.

Harcourt Brace School Publishers

NAME _____ DATE _____

YELLOWSTONE
National Park

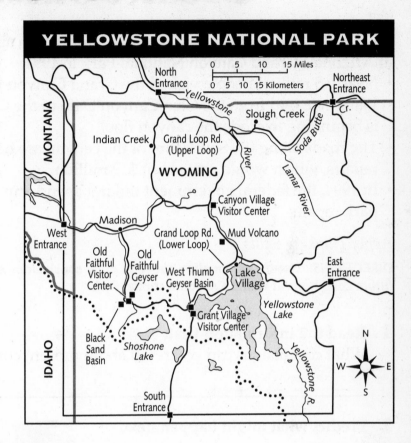

Map Skill

Apply Map Skills

DIRECTIONS: *Imagine that you are a park ranger at Yellowstone National Park. Use this map to answer the questions below.*

YELLOWSTONE NATIONAL PARK

0   5   10   15 Miles
0   5   10   15 Kilometers

North Entrance
Northeast Entrance
Yellowstone
Slough Creek
Soda Butte Cr.
MONTANA
Indian Creek
Grand Loop Rd. (Upper Loop)
WYOMING
Lamar River
River
Canyon Village Visitor Center
Madison
Grand Loop Rd. (Lower Loop)
Mud Volcano
West Entrance
Old Faithful Visitor Center
Old Faithful Geyser
West Thumb Geyser Basin
Lake Village
East Entrance
Grant Village Visitor Center
Yellowstone Lake
Black Sand Basin
Shoshone Lake
IDAHO
Yellowstone R.
South Entrance
N
W   E
S

1. Which park entrance is the nearest to Madison? _____

2. What is the name of the park's largest lake? _____

3. What is the Grand Loop? _____

_____

4. What sites will I pass traveling east from Madison around the Lower Loop to Old Faithful Geyser? Trace this route on the map.

_____

5. Grant Village Visitor Center is on what side of Yellowstone Lake?

_____

HOW TO FORM CONCLUSIONS AND Predict Outcomes

The following statements provide information about conditions in Arizona's Grand Canyon National Park in 1994.

- Nearly 5 million people visited the Grand Canyon in 1994.
- Water released from the Glen Canyon Dam of the Colorado River is beginning to erode the canyon floor.
- The roads along the South Rim of the canyon are badly in need of repairs, which would cost about $19 million.
- In 1994, the federal government did not spend any money for park repairs.

Apply Thinking Skills

DIRECTIONS: Use the information above to draw conclusions and predict possible future conditions at Grand Canyon National Park.

1. **Read the information first.**
What conclusions can you reach about present conditions at the park?

_____

2. **Predict what might happen next.**
If no repairs are made, what might conditions be like in a few years at the park?

_____

_____

3. **If possible, verify your prediction.**

_____

_____

_____

4. **If necessary, change or adjust your prediction.**

_____

Harcourt Brace School Publishers

Mountain Diaries

Apply Language Arts Skills

DIRECTIONS: Read the travel diary entries below. Each entry describes one of the mountain ranges listed on the right. Write the name of the correct mountain range under each diary entry.

the Alps
the Andes Mountains
the Atlas Mountains
the Himalayas

Today we visited the copper mines. On the way, we passed a group of women heading for market. The women wore brightly colored ponchos. They led llamas carrying heavy sacks of potatoes.

_____

Yesterday we saw some goats grazing among the dry rocks. We stood on a peak and looked out across the vast desert to the south.

_____

Yesterday we took a train that passed through a long tunnel under the mountains. We are staying in a small village where all the houses have sharply peaked roofs. We watched a dairy farmer send milk through a pipe that will carry it for miles down to the valley below.

_____

Today I saw some Sherpas harvesting rice on the mountain slopes. I don't know how they manage to survive in the world's highest mountains.

_____

The Western Mountains

Connect Main Ideas

DIRECTIONS: Use this organizer to show that you understand
how the chapter's main ideas are connected. Complete it
by writing two sentences about each main idea.

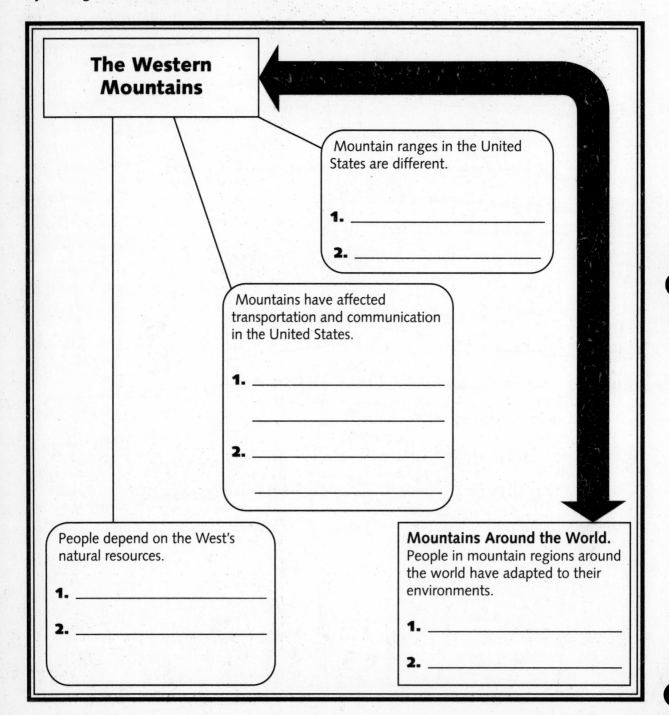

The Western Mountains

Mountain ranges in the United States are different.

1. _____

2. _____

Mountains have affected transportation and communication in the United States.

1. _____

   _____

2. _____

   _____

People depend on the West's natural resources.

1. _____

2. _____

Mountains Around the World.
People in mountain regions around the world have adapted to their environments.

1. _____

2. _____

Harcourt Brace School Publishers

The Western Ocean

Work with Vocabulary

DIRECTIONS: *Use the clues to fill in the words from 1 to 7. When you finish, read the letters inside the shaded squares from top to bottom to see the name of an ocean.*

1.

2.

3.

4.

5.

6.

7.

Clues

1. a large inlet in northwestern Washington State

2. a place American Indians called "ground on fire"

3. Indians who lived where the Columbia River meets the ocean

4. a metal used to make airplane parts

5. a narrow inlet of the ocean between cliffs

6. a group of pools of water built like steps to help fish get past a dam

7. the relationship between living things and their nonliving environment

HOW TO MAKE A Generalization

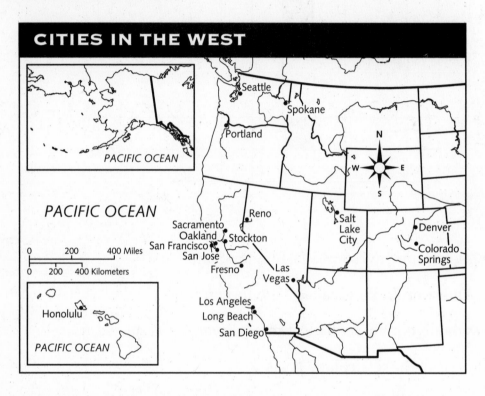

Map Skill *Apply Thinking Skills*

DIRECTIONS: The map below shows 18 of the largest cities in the West. Many of these cities are at the center of crowded metropolitan areas. Study the map, and then complete the activities that follow.

CITIES IN THE WEST

DIRECTIONS: Circle the number of the statements below that can be defended as generalizations based on the data presented in the map. On a separate sheet of paper, explain your responses.

1. The West is the most populated region in the United States.

2. Most of the large cities in the West are located on or near bodies of water.

3. California is the most populated state in the West.

4. Alaska is a heavily populated state.

ART of the NORTHWEST

American Indians who live along the Pacific coast, like the family in *Anna's Athabaskan Summer*, sometimes honor the animals and birds of their region in their artwork. Animal designs appear in small soapstone carvings or on large wooden totem poles. They are sewn onto clothing or woven into baskets.

Connect Art and Literature

DIRECTIONS: Draw a design for a basket using the animals, birds, and plants of your region. You can use the Northwest Indian designs on this page as models.

NAME _____ DATE _____

OIL SPILLS

Read a Table

DIRECTIONS: Use the table below to answer the questions that follow.

DATE	SHIP	PLACE WHERE SPILL OCCURRED	NUMBER OF BARRELS OF OIL SPILLED
March 1967	*Torrey Canyon*	English Channel	860,000
December 1976	*Argo Merchant*	Atlantic Ocean	180,000
March 1978	*Amoco Cadiz*	Atlantic Ocean	1,600,000
July 1979	*Atlantic Express* and *Aegean Captain*	Atlantic Ocean	2,100,000
November 1979	*Burmah Agate*	Galveston Bay	250,000
August 1983	*Castillo de Bellver*	Atlantic Ocean	1,750,000
March 1989	*Exxon Valdez*	Prince William Sound	260,000
February 1996	*Sea Empress*	Atlantic Ocean	476,000

1. According to the table, in what year did two major oil spills occur?

_____

2. Which oil spill was caused by the collision of two ships?

_____

3. Which ship was responsible for an oil spill in the English Channel?

_____

4. How did the spill caused by the *Exxon Valdez* compare to the spill caused by the *Amoco Cadiz*?

_____

_____

5. When did a large oil spill happen in Galveston Bay, in Texas? _____

Harcourt Brace School Publishers

Use after reading Chapter 13, Lesson 3, pages 426–430.

NAME _____ DATE _____

HOW TO ACT AS A Responsible Citizen

Apply Thinking Skills

DIRECTIONS: Read each of the following descriptions of a situation. Then choose one of the three situations. Answer the questions below, using the steps you learned for acting responsibly.

A. Every Saturday when you go to the park for soccer practice, you notice the same stray dog pawing through the garbage cans. Today you see some children teasing the dog.

B. You notice that a new classmate sits alone to eat lunch every day. The new student does not speak very much English.

C. At a playground, you see some children playing with firecrackers. They leave behind firecrackers and matches in an area where younger children often play.

1. What is the problem? _____

2. List some ways to solve the problem. _____

_____

_____

3. Is it safe to solve this problem yourself? Why or why not? If not, who can help you?

_____

_____

4. How would you solve the problem? Explain your decision.

_____

_____

_____

Harcourt Brace School Publishers

NAME _____ DATE _____

The State Seal of Hawaii

Analyze a State Seal

DIRECTIONS: *The seal of a state contains symbols that tell about the state. Study the state seal of Hawaii and the captions that explain it. Then answer the questions that follow.*

Pacific sunset

King Kamehameha I, who united the Hawaiian Islands in the 1700s

Phoenix, a legendary bird born in fire

The state motto: Hawaiian for "The life of the land is preserved in righteousness [justice]"

The year Hawaii became a state

The shield of Hawaii's royal family

Lady Liberty carrying Hawaii's state flag

Taro and banana leaves and maidenhair ferns, typical Hawaiian plants

1. What is the name of the king who is shown on the Hawaii state seal?

_____

2. When did Hawaii become a state? _____

3. Why do you think the seal includes a sunset? _____

4. Why do you think the seal shows a legendary bird that was born in fire?

_____

5. What items might you include if you were designing a new state seal for

your state? _____

DIRECTIONS: *On a separate sheet of paper, create a personal seal. Use drawings that tell about your personal history and things you like to do. Make sure to include your name and a personal motto (some words to live by).*

Use after reading Chapter 13, Lesson 4, pages 432–435.

Harcourt Brace School Publishers

NAME _____ DATE _____

HOW TO USE A MAP TO SHOW *Movement*

The Hawaiian Islands were originally bare volcanic rocks. All of its plants, animals, and birds came from other parts of the world. Many were brought by early explorers and settlers. The map below shows where some of Hawaii's plants, animals, and birds came from.

Apply Map Skills

DIRECTIONS: *Use the map to answer the questions that follow.*

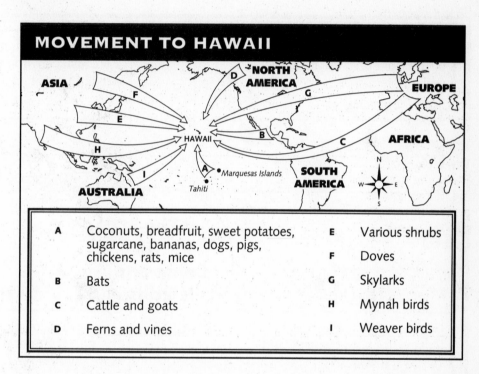

MOVEMENT TO HAWAII

A	Coconuts, breadfruit, sweet potatoes, sugarcane, bananas, dogs, pigs, chickens, rats, mice	**E**	Various shrubs
		F	Doves
B	Bats	**G**	Skylarks
C	Cattle and goats	**H**	Mynah birds
D	Ferns and vines	**I**	Weaver birds

1. From which direction did coconuts first reach Hawaii? _____

2. In which direction did doves travel to reach Hawaii? _____

3. Which animal traveled west from North America to reach Hawaii?

_____

4. From which continent did the weaver bird travel to reach Hawaii?

_____

5. What did Europe contribute to Hawaii's animal life?

_____

Harcourt Brace School Publishers

The Pacific Coast and Islands

Connect Main Ideas

DIRECTIONS: Use this organizer to show that you know how the chapter's main ideas are connected. Complete it by writing three examples to support each main idea.

Places along the Pacific coast of the United States are alike and different.

1. _____

2. _____

3. _____

People have both damaged the coastal environment and worked to protect it.

1. _____

2. _____

3. _____

The Pacific Coast and Islands

Life for Alaska's Athabaskan Indians has both changed and stayed the same.

1. _____

2. _____

3. _____

Hawaii's location has affected the state's history and the state's people.

1. _____

2. _____

3. _____

Harcourt Brace School Publishers

Use after reading Chapter 13, pages 412–437.